USA TODAY BESTSELLING AUTHOR

# Dale Mayer

# TERK'S GUARDIANS

## REID 06

REID: TERK'S GUARDIANS, BOOK 6
Beverly Dale Mayer
Valley Publishing Ltd.



ISBN-13: 978-1-778863-10-3
Print Edition

## Books in This Series:

# About This Book

Reid Cocheran is eager to see Venialla again, after losing contact years ago when they were in the same research group. Finding out that MI6 lost her and her mother in a secret operation, while moving them both back to England, has him volunteering immediately.

Veni Baronov and her mother were caught escaping Russia where her mother, more prisoner than employee, had been working for the government. This was their one chance at freedom—before her parents' employer discovered there was more to Veni than she wanted them … or anyone … to know.

Veni had always been independent, but sometimes a little help is needed. This time it will take a lot of help, especially now that MI6 had failed them. There is someone she can call on for help, but it requires skills she didn't dare use—not when others want to wield them against her …

**Sign up to be notified of all Dale's releases here!**
https://geni.us/DaleNews

TERKEL LOOKED OVER at Celia. "How many rooms do we have in this place?"

She burst out laughing. "It seems like hundreds, but we will obviously need to get more bedrooms ready and the plumbing updated in some of the other wings. Still, we have plenty of room for them."

"Besides," Calum noted, as he looked over at them, "you wanted a big team, a team we can draw on, a team who could handle having families and being a part of this. So we definitely need to find room for them."

At that, Cara walked into the room, her belly clearing the way in front of her.

Terkel looked at her and sighed. "Did we get any forward movement on people to help with day care?"

"Not just people to help with day care but we'll need … probably two nurses to work full-time," Celia replied. "Plus, we now have a new chef for the kitchen, so Mariana can relax a little more, and we hired more kitchen staff full-time as well. They'll come back and forth, leaving us at the end of the day, which I think is better."

"I like that too," Terk muttered. Just then his phone rang. He looked down at the screen and frowned. "Jonas, what's up?"

"What's up is that I have another job," he barked, his

tone grim. "Not exactly sure if this is your thing though."

"Even if it isn't, that doesn't mean we can't do it. We just have an extra edge on the market for something like this."

"It's time sensitive."

"It always is. What's up?"

"We had an Eastern Bloc research specialist coming over to England, and she's been kidnapped," he stated.

"Was she moving to England?"

"She was leaving her country. She was born over here, which apparently made the decision easier for her, but her parents emigrated over to Russia, and she was raised over there. She has traveled fairly extensively throughout the world, but the Russian government decided she's too dangerous to let out, that she knows too much, and she's way too skilled to let the Western world have her, so we worked hard to get her free. To our dismay, she's just been snagged out of Belgium," he shared. "We're still trying to get details, but I need a team, and I need a team now."

"Got it," Terk replied. "What doctor is this?"

"It's not just the doctor herself. It's her daughter as well."

"The daughter was kidnapped? How old is she?"

"She's twenty-six. She worked with her mother and apparently has some of the skills that you guys have. That's another reason why the mother was trying to get her out of there because the government was starting to make noise about keeping the doctor and her daughter there for their own secret programs."

"Of course they were," Terkel muttered, with an ugly frown. "I need details, but I've already got somebody here who can go."

"Good," Jonas said. "Glad to hear you're getting more

people. I wouldn't have thought you had such a large pool to draw from."

"This is someone who contacted me a few days ago. Obviously I have to call and confirm, but that's my problem, not yours."

When he ended that call, he quickly dialed Reid Cocheran. When Reid answered, Terk announced, "I've got a job for you, Reid."

"Good, I was getting a little bored."

"Where are you?"

"Switzerland."

"You're heading for Belgium," Terkel declared, and he mentioned the microbiologist.

"Oh hell," Reid replied, "that's Veni's family."

"Veni?"

"Yes, her name is Venialla, but she goes by Veni."

"You already know her?" Terk asked.

"We've met. I belong to a large group that she was involved with in terms of psychic work," Reid explained. "You get a large group of people who like to think they can do what we can do, but really can't. Like me, she popped in there to see if she found any people like her. The two of us connected, but I don't think very many others in the group were of any real value in terms of psychic skills. If I had thought there were, I would have told you about them already. So, in the meantime, she was looking to head back to the Western world again. I wasn't sure if that would work out. I lost track of her about eight months or so ago."

"Guess what? She resurfaced with MI6 agents who were trying to move her and her mother back to England, but now they've gone missing."

"Okay, I'm on it. Send me the deets. I'm already packed up, ready to go."

# CHAPTER 1

R EID PULLED HIS rental car into a back alley and off to the side, shut down the engine, and grabbed his phone. It had been buzzing with messages for the last little bit, but the traffic had been intense, with some carnival going on. So he remained focused on driving and not hurting anybody. As he quickly flicked through the messages, he was surprised at how quickly things had evolved around him. Apparently Anders, who was part of Levi's team, would help Reid on this one. He frowned at that. It was one thing to work for Terk, but he did remember Levi, assuming it was the same Levi.

He quickly texted Terk and asked. When Terk phoned him directly, his words were, "Yes, that's Levi."

"Fine. So this is one of his guys?"

"Yes, Anders has worked for Levi for quite a while. He was over in Europe anyway, which is what made him the ideal man right now. His family's gone back alone, their holiday over, so he'll give you a hand."

"You think I need a hand?"

"Yes," Terk confirmed, his tone terse. "I don't know who else I've got to send to you right now, who else is close by," Terk explained. "So we'll give you some ground support this way."

"Ground support—if it's the kind I think of—is probably more valuable than anything Anders can do."

"Granted, you transmitters need a good grounding partner to aid your gift, and Anders doesn't have that skill. However, I wouldn't count him out. Levi's guys are experienced and have other skills, and they know what they're doing. If nothing else, it's always good to have somebody around to back you up."

"I won't argue with that," Reid admitted, then groaned. "However, it'll slow me down if I have to wait for him to reach me."

"I highly suspect you won't have to wait for long," Terk stated, with a note of humor. "And, if you get out of your vehicle now, you'll likely see him. So you are slowing yourself down." With a chuckle, Terk ended the call.

Startled, Reid hopped out of his vehicle and turned to look. Indeed, a man strode toward him, coming up the alleyway. Reid studied the confident posture and the power that man emanated.

When the stranger came before Reid, barely a smile was given, but he gave him a nod. "Reid?"

"Yes. I gather you're Anders."

"I am. Let's go. We're out of time."

Surprised at that, but agreeing nonetheless, Reid hopped back into the vehicle, started it, and asked, "Have you got a destination?"

"I figured we would start where they went missing, unless you have anything else in mind." And though the question was innocent, Anders's gaze was searching.

"No, I haven't got any insights as to where she is—or they," he corrected. "Yet I'm happy to have anybody else's view on that."

"I don't have *those* kinds of insights," Anders admitted,

chewing on *those* just a little too long, "I just understand humanity and what makes it tick."

"That's more than most of us do," Reid muttered.

At that, Anders cracked a smile. "Absolutely. According to Terk, you're one of his."

"I am, although I haven't necessarily started working for him."

"I don't think anybody *starts* working for Terk," Anders shared, with a smirk. "It seems you just get naturally drafted because of your abilities."

"Yeah? What about those who don't want to be drafted?" Reid asked, shooting Anders a glance, as he pulled back onto the main street.

"Then you don't. Though I've yet to see anybody *not* join Terk's team. Although it's fairly new as a private firm, but, after the problems they had, I know they don't take on just anybody."

"None of us do," Reid agreed. "I presume you mean the attack that they survived."

"That's exactly what I mean." He nodded. "It's one thing to be attacked. It's another thing to barely survive an attempt at complete annihilation by your own government."

"Yet we've all seen it."

"Unfortunately, it happens a little too often," Anders murmured.

"How long have you been with Levi?"

"A while."

Short, succinct, and that was it. That was all Anders said. Reid cracked a smile. "So you're here for the duration on this one?"

"I am." Then he cracked a smile himself, glanced at Reid, and added, "Whether you want me here or not."

Reid winced. "I'm really not used to working with anybody."

"Get used to it, because Terk's teams are pretty involved all over the world, one way or another, and these kind of joint team ops happen all the time, even if just two men."

"Again we're back to that part about *if I so choose.*"

"Yep, if you so choose," Anders repeated, "but the growth and development of the abilities of everybody on Terk's team—even those who didn't have what they would've considered abilities prior to joining—has been pretty amazing."

"Including you?" Reid asked.

At that, Anders gave a shout of laughter. "No." He shook his head. "I see black, and I see white, and there's not a whole lot in between, particularly not the grays that Terk walks. I've known him for a very long time though, and I know he's a straight shooter. If anybody else were to tell me that all this was possible, I would have called him a liar and then walked out of the room."

"Yeah, I understand," Reid stated, "and I've met guys like you before. Thankfully Terk appears to have a lot of influence all over the world."

"Once you start dealing with him, it's hard to forget—or to dismiss your brand of skills," he admitted. "He's also not a bullshitter, and that we can all respect. If he gets his information from sources that none of us really want to contemplate, well, that's fine with me too. At least he uses the information to help others, and, in our case, he has saved several of our team members. He's assisted us multiple times, so we don't really argue what we cannot understand. Besides, his brother is a good man as well, and I would trust him to watch my back anytime."

"I've never met Merk," Reid admitted, "but apparently they're quite close."

"They are definitely close," Anders agreed. "I'm not sure how you could help it when your brother can read your every thought."

"They must have worked out a system where he doesn't get to do that," Reid suggested, "because, when you don't want your thoughts read, and people do it anyway, it causes all kinds of hell."

"Sure it does, but they seem to manage. And that's where the agreement and the respect cooperate, where somebody gets to draw that line. However, Terk does cross it, when he has to."

"And I will too," Reid stated. "If I feel the need because I know there's danger, I will too." At that, Anders glared at him. Reid just shrugged. "We all must learn and grow. You signed on for the job, so, for me, that means you do as well."

"Put all that aside and let's go find the last spot where they were seen." And, with that, he punched the address into the GPS, and they headed off.

VENI BARONOV SQUINTED and stared at the scene in front of her. Her brain tried to process the situation, trying to make sense of the craziness of all that had just gone wrong in her world. Part of her brain still fought the drugs, and another part tried to sort out what was happening.

Something told her not to move, no matter what. She froze her neck, holding it still, not moving in the slightest, yet she had no idea why. As she slowly engaged all her senses, she confirmed that she was in the back of a van, her hands tied, a gag in her mouth. Right beside her, directly in her field of vision, was her mother, her beautiful, talented mother. She was unconscious and bouncing back and forth, as they took hard corners.

Veni was jammed up against a solid surface, with a bag or something behind her, so she wasn't feeling the effects of the vehicle's erratic movements quite so severely. Yet watching her mother bounce around so freely was painful. She wanted to reach for her, but she also knew that was futile. Her instincts told her, *Don't move, don't shift, don't cry out, don't do anything.* She took a slow, deep breath, trying to calm the panic in her heart, as her brain filtered the memories back in, reminding her of what had happened.

Veni and her mother had been on their way to England, defecting back to their home country. Both women had been born there to a Russian father, which influenced their birth names and eventual travel plans back to Russia. Veni's parents had split years ago, yet both her mom and dad still worked for the Russian government. Veni did too, after her college years—only to be more prisoner than employee. Veni wasn't free to do any of the work she wanted to do. Her parents weren't free to choose their projects either, but they seemed okay with that. Veni sighed. Everything required permission. Somewhere along the line someone had told the Russian government too much …

Maybe due to Veni's own foolishness from years ago. She thought she'd wiped clean her entire history, but, when you're young and stupid, you don't think about whether your presence in a forum a decade ago would make such a ruckus. However, the opposite became true for Veni. The Russian government believed Veni was capable of doing things far more advanced than anything she was willing to let them know about. The fact that she hadn't let them know of these things was all the more horrible—in the eyes of the Russians—and yielded more strikes against her.

Veni had truly hidden things from them, yet they made too much of her rusty and unwieldy skill. That discovery and Russia's reaction to it had led to her mother's decision. *Both* of them had made the decision together, so Veni couldn't solely blame her mother for it. Veni had been just as desperate to get out of the country and to find a place where she could be safe. However, she wouldn't leave without her mom, and her mother wouldn't go it alone.

Especially not if that involved leaving Veni behind.

Her father, as she'd eventually come to realize, didn't have their best interests at heart. That fact was difficult for her mother to accept, until she finally accepted that to stay was to forfeit any kind of a happy life for her daughter. That had been the impetus they needed to make the contacts and to start the painful and scary wait, while secret plans were set in motion.

Obviously whatever plans had been made were discovered and blocked. So here Veni was, once again a captive, and, based on the language spoken in the front of the vehicle, back in Russian hands. At that point, her mom moaned ever-so-softly. Veni's hands were tied, so all she could do was send out good vibes, as much as her still-drugged brain would allow, hoping to somehow soothe her mom, praying her mother would be quiet, would stay calm, and wouldn't give up just yet.

Veni wasn't sure what the new plan would be going forward. She didn't have one, if the truth be told, but she needed to find one and find one soon. Their kidnappers were driving them somewhere, but that journey could end at any moment. Veni needed an escape plan because the last thing she would do was go back under Russian rule. Not when they wanted her to do just that and only that.

Her mother moaned again.

Veni heard swearing from the front seat of the vehicle, with the driver proceeding at a fast pace down a highway. Veni could only hope their kidnappers didn't hear her mother. In the recesses of Veni's mind, she knew it would be bad if they did. She shifted ever-so-slightly, hoping to reach for her mother's hand to comfort her, but Veni couldn't quite make it.

When her mother moaned yet again, somebody in the front swore again, and Veni listened to the murmuring back and forth. Finally she made out something.

"I don't give a crap how you do it. Shut her up."

Veni winced at that because her mom would get the brunt of that order, but, if the men also knew Veni was awake, she would be targeted as well. She allowed herself to sink heavily back into a drugged state, to relax her facial muscles, knowing when one tried to appear to be asleep or unconscious, it didn't always work. In her case, allowing the haze of the drugs to return, she could hope that it would.

She heard sounds, as somebody moved from the front seat into the back of the vehicle. Veni waited, her eyelids shut, until she heard a rustle nearby. Then taking a chance, she slitted her eyelids to see one of the men shoving a needle into her mother's arm.

Veni's heart sank, knowing that would keep her mother unconscious for hours, right at the very time when Veni might have been able to get them out of here, both alert and mobile—if only her mom had woken up early enough herself, without these guys knowing about it.

Just then the man called out to the driver, "What about the other one?"

"If she's not awake, don't give her more," he cautioned.

"You sure about that?"

"We don't want to give her more if she's still unconscious. We could end up hurting her." His tone had turned hard, as if annoyed at having to repeat the instructions.

"Yeah, well, if what they say she can do is accurate, I wouldn't mind hurting her myself."

"That's not the point," he replied. "Remember how the boss is pretty adamant that we get them back into the labs really quick, without hurting the bitches unnecessarily."

"Okay, fine. I'll leave her for now. She looks pretty out of it."

"Good. Not that I trust her, particularly that one."

"Maybe I should inject her anyway then."

"No, just leave it. I don't want to be the guy who has to tell the boss that we killed her."

"Right, that wouldn't be good for anybody, would it?" With a half laugh he already made his way back to the front of the van.

She sighed with relief that she wouldn't get another shot, so maybe she could function enough to find a way out of this mess. Besides, if her brain was operating correctly, maybe she could send out telepathic messages.

"How come we're not concerned about her contacting people with her mind, if that's what she can do?"

"I don't know, but they did something to her that's supposed to stop it."

"Really?" Surprise was evident in his tone. "Man, I never thought I would see the day where we could do things like that. Pretty awesome."

"I don't know about *awesome*," his partner noted, "but she's dangerous. It's not natural to do something like that."

While the men carried on with their trash talk, Veni froze, wondering just what the hell they had done to her to stop her abilities. Was it permanent, or was it just another nightmare testing scenario, something they were mulling over, trying it, seeing if it would work? Her vote was that such a thing would never work, but that's because she didn't want to believe they had any way to stop her abilities, especially her telepathic communications with other gifted persons in the world. As she lay here, she considered that their intercession might have worked, since all her efforts to reach out to those she knew just hit a wall, a blank wall.

She was afraid she knew what that meant.

She was way too tired to keep fighting the drugs, whatever she had been given was still running rampant in her system. As the driver turned hard at another corner, she shifted abruptly and hit her head with enough force that she slowly sank back into unconsciousness.

# CHAPTER 2

V ENI WOKE WITH a hell of a headache, noting she was still in the back of the van. Maybe the same van, maybe a different one? She had no way to know. It was difficult to get her brain to function properly; everything was glazed, as if coming from a long distance away. Her eyesight wasn't even working the way she would have liked. Instantly she was terrified that something was seriously wrong, but *seriously* and *wrong* were not the same thing when it came to this kind of nightmare. Obviously something was very wrong. The problem at hand was to figure out who did what to her and how the hell it all came to be.

She already knew part of it, and the most important thing was figuring out what she would do about it. That was still a question. She sent out yet another message to anybody close enough to hear, and, once again, it bounced back. Her kidnappers had already mentioned using some technology to keep her from successfully sending messages. That was when they didn't even know what she could do, so it worried her gravely that they had somehow managed to find a way to stop her.

What could she expect when they figured out more of what she could do?

Just then the side door of the van opened, startling her, and she turned to her mother, only to find herself all alone in the van. Her opportunity to escape free and clear had come and gone, before she'd even recognized it.

"Look at that. There you are and wide awake too," said the grinning man, missing a front tooth. "Welcome back to Russia."

Her heart sank at that, and she screamed mentally. *Please, no, please don't let it be true. Not back to the same place I fought so hard to get out of.*

Then, as if he had heard her, he changed his wording slightly. "Not quite yet but we'll be there soon."

As she stared at him mutely, he continued to smile. "You should never have tried to run. Now you'll pay the price."

"*Right*, as if I wasn't paying the price already," she muttered, but the gag made her words a garbled mess. It didn't matter at all, as her guard didn't care what she said.

When he pulled her to her feet, her knees buckled instantly.

"*Tsk, tsk, tsk.* Fools. I guess they didn't let you exercise your legs at all, did they?" he asked, with a sigh. "It'll take you a few days to get over this. They never think about their prisoners."

She didn't think anybody ever thought about their prisoners, and those two hadn't been interested in anything but getting the job done. All they'd been concerned about was getting back, before they got into trouble for having lost them to begin with. And just now, if she'd been a bit more alert, she could have made a run for it. Yet not without her mom. Still, judging from the weakness of her legs, not to mention her mind, Veni could only do so much right now. Therefore, it seemed as if she couldn't do very much of anything under these circumstances. That damn wall was closing all around her, and the realization brought hot tears to her eyes. She struggled to shake them off, hating that she still ended up teary-eyed in the midst of trauma.

But her guard seemed to take no notice of her emotional state, only her physical reaction. "That's just the drugs."

Such a comfortable rumble filled his tone that those words almost seemed rote for him, as if he did this on a regular basis—reassuring his prisoners, so they wouldn't be even more terrified than they already were. Russia had a bad name for many things, but something you could always do was buy anything you wanted, … if you had enough money. Such deals were always done through the gangs and secret organizations, but nobody cared, just as long as each party to the transaction kept quiet and didn't make a big scene. Of course most people involved in this particular cash market didn't want to reveal anything because, whatever they were doing, they were doing for profit, and apparently a lot of profit could be had.

Not that she knew anything about that until now, and she couldn't waste any time trying to figure it out either. She must remain focused on trying to save her own sorry skin and that of her mother. Veni certainly hadn't expected her own father to turn them in. *If* he had turned them in. That was her instinctive answer to how they ended up in this situation, but she didn't really know.

But she would find out, at all costs. She had promised herself that, no matter what happened, somehow she would discover whoever had turned them in. The thought that this attempt had gone so seriously wrong was heartbreaking because there shouldn't have been an opportunity for anybody to betray them. Their escape should have been locked up tight, as she'd expected it to be. Simple, clean-cut, a precise surgical attack. So what had happened? And how would she and her mother ever get out this?

If these guys had their way, she would never get out of the prison they would put her in. *Forever*, that was her sentence, and she knew it. The Russian government couldn't afford not to jail her in effect, particularly if they had determined that she had any special skills that she could *lend* to their organizations. Whether she did or not wasn't something she was prepared to discuss. Not to these guys. That conversation would not be happening anytime soon. Or ever.

Everybody always wanted something from her, and it was enough to break her heart. All she really wanted was to get back to England and to find a way to make herself a life again. A normal life, with people who knew who she was, what she was. A life where she felt at home, instead of being persecuted, kidnapped, and imprisoned for someone's little pet projects, where they got to test her like a lab rat.

At the moment though, it looked as though her one chance at freedom had been a bust.

REID PARKED OUTSIDE the commercial building, and he and Anders walked up to the front door.

"I've got a question for you," Anders began, as they studied their surroundings, both men vigilant and on edge.

"Yeah, what is it?"

"If she's got these abilities, how come she's not sending you any, … I don't know, signals, signs, or whatever? Normally Terk can pick up on somebody like this."

Reid looked over at him and nodded. "Normally, yes, that's true. Which means that, if Terk can't, we have to assume the worst."

At that, Anders' eyebrows shot up. "She's dead?"

"I would think that we would know that big of a detail already, but it's possible. I was thinking more along the lines that maybe she's unconscious or heavily drugged, which is about the only way for them to still or to hinder her subconscious mind. If they have another method, that's bad news for her and for us as well."

"Meaning, if something like that could be used against her, chances are it could also be used against you, Terk, and, well, the whole team."

"Exactly. They've already come up against a couple people doing their darndest to stop them from doing what we do," Reid noted.

Anders nodded at that. "I didn't hear the full story, but I heard enough."

"And *enough* is all we ever really need to understand the kind of hell that our enemies are trying to rain down on us," he muttered.

Anders smiled and said, "But we're on this."

"We *are* on it, but the very question you asked me is the one I've been trying to answer myself. What would it take for her to *not* contact us? And honestly I don't like my options. The answer most likely suggests that she's incapable of it, and, therefore, she's either heavily drugged or, … or maybe so badly injured that she can't get past the pain and the hurt in order to contact us."

"Is it possible to get past that kind of pain?"

He gave him a small smile and a curt nod. "Yes, but it's not easy."

With that, they rang the bell and waited, not expecting anybody to be here. It would be better if nobody answered, so they could go in and have a look around.

As he studied the building, Anders asked, "What's the deal with this place anyway?"

Reid pulled out his phone and looked at the information he'd been given by Terk. "An old warehouse. They're still trying to track down ownership. Veni was seen being escorted outside over there." He turned and pointed at the building across the road. "According to the info we were sent, she was led here."

"And her mother?"

"And her mother. They were both walked across the road here and into this building."

"So it's likely they used it as a holding spot."

"That's what it seems to be to me," Reid muttered.

"Yet that is an interesting location. I presume Terk or the Levi-Ice duo are doing some sort of rundown on it?"

"Absolutely they are," Reid confirmed, "but, so far, outside of the fact that this warehouse has been vacant for the last three years, nobody knows who may have discovered its lack of tenants and put it to use for themselves. Yet you and I both know it doesn't take much to make that kind of connection. It's easily done. Once a place is empty for any length of time, squatters of whatever sort take it over, then all bets are off. Lots of people could be using this space for their own. As long as they keep that information close, nobody cares. Once they start causing trouble and bring it to somebody's attention, then things go awry. These empty buildings are used all over the world, and that is just a fact. It doesn't make me feel any better, though."

Anders nodded. "It would be nice if we could find some connection to it, though," he muttered. "If there is one, we can trust Ice, Levi, and the team to find it," Anders stated.

"This right here is definitely their kind of thing."

"You mean, *your* kind of thing?" Reid asked, eyeing Anders curiously.

"Yeah, absolutely," he murmured, then looked around. "I'm not sure whether you're with me or not, but I'll take a walk inside." And, with that, he picked the lock quickly and stepped in, with a look at Reid behind him.

Since that was exactly what Reid had planned on doing, he followed Anders. Inside, they closed the door and surveyed the space. He wasn't sure what Anders was looking for, but Reid was looking for energy signatures. As he opened up his vision to see just what had been going on in here, he was immediately slammed by way more energy than he could process. With a hard groan, he slammed shut his senses and sucked in his breath, trying to calm himself down from the onslaught.

"You want to explain that?" Anders asked at his side.

"If you don't ask too many questions, yeah," he conceded, with a wry sigh. "I opened my energy to see what signatures, energy signatures, I would find in this place. Unfortunately this place has been heavily used, and it's full of energy, so I was caught off guard by the sheer amount and power of it. All of which means it'll be much harder for me to find out who was here and the purpose for this building." At the look Anders gave in response, Reid's lips twitched. "Right, woo-woo stuff," Reid confirmed, then snickered. "I guess that's something you guys aren't … terribly comfortable with."

"I'm pretty comfortable with what I can see and hear and touch," Anders declared, "but beyond that? Well, you're asking a lot from somebody who doesn't deal in woo-woo."

"Hey, you're the one who asked," Reid noted.

At that, Anders just nodded and didn't say anything.

As they quickly searched the building, Reid stepped back a little bit and announced, "I'll try again."

Anders nodded and waited.

This time, Reid opened up his senses a little bit at a time, which gave him the ability to filter in some energy at a slower rate than others, until he could open his gaze fully and then stare around the room. "A good twenty to thirty energies, well, twenty, twenty-five maybe, are here," he clarified. "That means they have used this space on a regular basis."

"*Huh.*"

"But it's not coming across as fresh energy."

"Okay, but this place, … it *was* a working business at one time, so that would make sense."

Reid had to give Anders kudos because he didn't ask questions or argue. He just accepted the information as presented. Reid could really appreciate working with somebody who trusted his partner at that level. Not that trust was really involved at this point, but, hey, Reid wasn't being slammed with derision, and he would take that any day. "But," Reid added, turning toward the opposite wall, his breath catching in the back of his throat, "Veni was here."

"Where?" Anders asked, all business.

Reid pointed to the corner, walking closer. "She was here. She entered via the front door and was parked in this corner."

"This is pretty public," Anders pointed out, turning to look around. "Very public, as in she was kept in plain sight. That doesn't make much sense."

"Kept in plain sight, quite possibly drugged or injured at

this point," Reid shared. "There is violence in the air, but I'm not really getting a measure on how it was meted out." Anders once again shot him an odd look, but Reid ignored it. "I am getting a lot of confusion, as if Veni doesn't know what's going on or why. Then there's fear, but it's not prevalent."

"Why wouldn't it be though?" Anders asked curiously. "You would think she would be terrified."

"Probably mostly because she was part of the plan to get out and knew what was happening. She just doesn't know who did the job and what became of it."

"Do you think this was part of the plan? To take her here?"

Reid frowned. "I don't think the plan was to take her specifically here. I think this was a holding area because whatever snatch-and-grab the kidnappers did was successful, and this was a way to work out the second part of their plan. Just ..." His phone buzzed at that point. He looked down to see a message from Terk. "Shit." He turned to Anders. "The two Russian escorts she had were just found."

"As in?" Anders asked.

"Their bodies were recovered, floating in a small river."

Anders muttered, "Of course. That means they were taken out and dumped. Which means that the Russians are really serious about keeping these women."

"*Very* serious at this point, I would say," Reid stated, refusing to let his mind go in the obvious direction.

"Still," Anders went on, "it's also possible the women now have new kidnappers, and the players have changed. We assumed the Russian government had gone after them, but we don't know if that's changed."

Reid groaned. "The only good thing about this is knowing that both women are valuable to the Russians, as in seriously valuable. So chances are good they will want them alive."

Anders nodded in agreement. "If these two women can do anything along the lines of what you and Terk can do, that makes perfect sense. I've never quite understood how Terk stayed safe all these years."

"Part of it was the fact that our government kept their skill sets a big secret, keeping what they could do on the down low. They didn't want anybody knowing about Terk and what he could do either. Now that Terk and his team are free and clear, they still basically work for governments, a few different ones now," Reid explained. "So I don't think anybody is ready to brace them again, especially not if they know the story of how Terk and his team survived that awful attack."

"True, but some egomaniac out there would like to test you guys, I'm sure. So you always wonder if it won't happen someday."

"Yep," Reid murmured. "I feel as if Terk's team has discussed that, and everybody is prepared to do what they need to do. Yet they want a chance to live a normal life, whatever that's worth or even means."

"Does it have a meaning when it comes to you guys?" Anders asked, with a sigh. "It seems as if Terk's always been chasing shadows, and now he's got people who are important to him, people he cares about—a family, a wife. I guess I'm surprised that he's still doing what he's doing."

"He's always had people who are important to him. His team was his first family, from what I hear. He takes pretty good care of his team and always has. I think you'll find that he's doing what he's doing to keep everyone alive. Terk isn't the only one with a wife now. A good share of the team is partnered up, one way or another, and I don't even know how many babies are on the way. Terk does what he does to ensure they're on top of their game, so that he can keep them in all good shape, plus keep them strong and active in the industry. That way he knows what's going on—instead of being blindsided, the way they were the last time. Staying isolated doesn't end well."

"That makes more sense." Anders nodded. "If you think about it, you have to keep your enemies close."

"As the saying goes, *keep your friends close and your enemies closer*," Reid clarified. "In this case, I highly suspect that a trusted friend in Veni's world betrayed them in the end, and that will be hard for her to handle too."

"It has to be," Anders agreed. "Betrayal is always hard, but, when it comes from inside your closest circle, it's the worst, and unfortunately it happens way too often."

With one final check they walked out of the building, searching their surroundings. Reid sent a text message to Terk, asking if they checked all the street cams in the area around the building.

Terk phoned him. "Did you find anything inside?"

"Not really, except energy confirmation that Veni was here. She was kept in the corner, where everybody coming and going could see her."

"Either as a prize or to keep her under control?"

"Probably both. There was … pain and some degree of fear in her energy. I'm not thinking that she's seriously hurt, but I don't have any proof of that. She was definitely drugged though. She was *walking through a cloud* while she was here."

"All of that makes sense," Terk noted a bit too harshly.

"I'm not sure where to send you next."

"I'll take a walk around the exterior of the building and see if I can find her energy again, just in case we've missed something," Reid shared, disconnecting from Terk and passing the information to Anders. "I want to check out the perimeter of the building."

"I'm coming too."

Reid nodded. "Probably best if we stay together anyway."

"Any particular reason?" Anders asked.

He gave him a crooked smile. "Yeah, because the Russians have a tendency to shoot first and to ask questions later," he explained, "and it would be nice if I had somebody to back me up."

"That's what I'm here for," Anders said cheerfully. "Can't say I particularly want to get shot on this job, so I'll do my best to avoid it too. Yet it is that kind of a job."

"Apparently. And the fact that they kidnapped and drugged a twenty-six-year-old woman and her mother is despicable."

"Yeah, and what I really don't understand is who would have done it and why. I mean, it seems the Russians had her first, but there may have been an interruption or a handoff, right? We definitely need a full history."

Reid asked, "Don't you already have it? It should have been in your inbox already."

"Sure, I read it on the way over," Anders confirmed, "but it was incomplete, and I have questions. Like, what is your relationship with her? What are her abilities, and how is it that somebody could make use of them against her will? I need anything that you've got to share."

"Sure, just ask me. I met her during college, parted ways,

but kept in touch here and there. Then I lost track of her months ago. Her mother can be used as the perfect leverage to get Veni to do pretty much anything. She's a transmitter, a very strong one. Plus she's pretty good at determining whether someone is lying or telling the truth," he added, with a wry smile. "She can basically just look at you, register the energy, and say, *Yeah, bullshit.*"

At that, Anders stared at him, eyebrows raised. "I can see where that would be very helpful for several types of businesses." He considered that for a moment. "Yeah, I suppose any government would really like to have that in their arsenal, wouldn't they?"

"Absolutely. Though in her case, she has a fairly no-bullshit style about her and calls out people when they're lying. I also know that she can sometimes send out messages, which adds to her value. She's a transmitter but not a confident receiver, so, as long as she's sending messages, we may get a location on her. Yet she won't call out to Terk and ask for help because she can't receive messages on her own."

"How is that even possible? I mean, that's like giving somebody a car but not giving them the ability to drive. I mean, you need both halves of a talent like that, correct?"

"It certainly would help, yes," Reid muttered. "However, nobody really cares about why we have our abilities. It is what it is, and, while we all know our gifts can evolve, that is not the topic of this discussion."

"Do you mean they can really change over time?"

"They can. They can grow, and they can certainly be developed. Lately Terk has seen them change at a much faster rate. Certainly in Terk's case, as each team member came back after being injured, they had all grown at a pretty crazy rate," Reid shared. "And part of me is kind of jealous.

Yet I really don't want to go through what they went through in order to get there."

At that, Anders burst out laughing, as they walked around to the back of the building. "No, I don't imagine you do," he noted, "but, if it gave Terk a lot more abilities, and it'll help keep him safe, I'm all for it."

"Oh, it will definitely do more to keep him safe. He can also talk to more people. His ability to empower others is also huge," Reid added, "which is one of the reasons why I would consider moving over there. I've been footloose and fancy-free, but then you start to wonder if there isn't more for you, if there isn't more you could be doing. And those guys over at Terk's team are doing it, so a part of me would very much like to check that out."

"Let's get this job done first," Anders noted, "and then you can go play house in that crazy castle full of all those children they've got coming along."

"I know, right?" Reid laughed. "Can't say I would mind being around kids either. A lot of joy in that."

"What about kids who have the same abilities?" Anders asked, staring at him. "No way Terk's kids won't be gifted. I understand Terk's wife has energy skills too."

"It can happen, and that'll be one of those things they'll have to look at—making sure the kids are welcome and valued, regardless of whatever abilities they have. However, I don't think that will be a problem with Terk. He would probably say they were lucky to be born into a gifted family because they wouldn't be tormented by the nightmares and voices in his head at all hours the way Terk had gone through all by himself. And yet Merk, his brother, doesn't have any of those woo-woo skills, which I always found strange."

"Yep, and Merk is one of my best friends," Anders shared. "I understand his frustration sometimes too. I know that his brother was tormented constantly, so Merk didn't really want anything to do with it."

"The psychic opportunity is probably still there for Merk, if he ever wanted to open that door," Reid suggested.

"I think Terk may have mentioned that a time or two, and Merk's always just shot him down. I don't think that door is one he ever wants to open."

"It's not for everyone," Reid agreed, looking over at Anders. "Just knowing something is about to go down is one thing, but then to find out you can't do anything to change such an outcome is pretty devastating. That's something we deal with constantly."

"Yet Veni doesn't deal with that, does she?"

"Nope. For her, it was more of a party game, at least until whatever happened to her, that thereafter set her on this path."

"I wonder what that was."

"I don't know. I haven't had any *personal* contact with her in a couple years. Yet I've always searched online for her at times to see what she's been up to," he admitted. "I knew that her family was living in Russia, and I had always hoped that she was trying to get out. Yet I didn't realize that things were desperate enough that something like this was in the cards. For her to have participated in an escape attempt like this, instead of just trying to sneak out, means that it was serious, and sneaking away wasn't an option.

"So that says to me, if she couldn't just sneak out, someone was controlling her life, and she must have been terrified of them. And that is something I'll have a hard time forgiving myself for not seeing the signs. Veni comes from the heart. She's a good person. If she can help you, she will, and, if she can't, she's a no-bullshit type person. So she won't, and she'll tell you why.

"Yet to think of somebody hurting her, simply because she can tell whether somebody tells the truth or lies, that's a little hard to handle. However, I also know how governments feel about things like that. So, if she has those gifts and potentially more, she's an asset they can't afford to let anybody else have, even if they don't want it for themselves."

At that, Anders looked at Reid and nodded. "It could be just as simple as that. The Russians are scared that what she might do is more than what she's let them know about. So essentially they're afraid of whatever she *can* do, and they might be afraid that the West could utilize them against Russia."

# CHAPTER 3

THE SOUND REVERBERATED across the room. Veni's head spun, as she groaned back to awareness, her cheek on fire, as she stared balefully at the man who had struck her.

"There you are," he greeted her, with a smile. "See? You cooperate with me, and I'll cooperate with you."

She blinked, trying to clear her head once again, knowing that the dizziness came from the drugs they kept putting into her system. Drugs were the death knell for somebody like her, but these guys didn't care. As long as it made her more cooperative, they were all for it. That just added more to her pain, not that they cared. It was all about them and what they wanted. She closed her eyes again, earning another slap across the face.

"I said, wake up," he snarled.

She blinked several times, wincing at the sting on her cheek and at the pounding in her head.

"That's more like it. Now stay awake or ..." he threatened. He studied her, as she gave in to her urge to sleep. "Do I have to hit you again?"

Slowly she shook her head. Her mouth was bound with a gag, her hands and feet were tied in front of her, and her body would soon scream in agony now that she was conscious. Not that he would mind.

"I brought you food and water," he stated, quickly untying the gag around her mouth. He handed her the water bottle, and she drank greedily. Almost immediately he pulled it back and glared at her. "Drink it slowly."

She noted this was the same man missing a tooth, who had seemed almost fatherly before, but that persona was long gone. Now she was dealing with this monster, who cared about nothing but making her follow whatever orders he gave. Guys like that were always around, happier to beat and to abuse than to be decent human beings. She shouldn't be surprised that the Russian government had hired somebody like this. Probably the regular government staff was around, the people nobody ever got to know about, yet they were here nonetheless. She slowly sipped at her drink, afraid that he would snatch it away from her again.

She knew she needed to drink slowly. Otherwise she would throw up. She would also need a bathroom thereafter, which she wasn't sure whether they would offer or not. Even now, as the water went in, she felt her other bodily systems rising up. She handed him the bottle and whispered, "I need to go to the bathroom."

He nodded. "It's about time," he muttered. "You should have gone a long time ago. I was starting to get worried," he declared, almost in disgust. "Get up."

She frowned at him, slowly getting to all fours, then to her knees, struggling to stand, as both her feet and her hands were still bound. But she made it to a vertical position, swaying a bit, slowly gaining control.

"Good, you're doing better than I expected." He quickly cut the bindings on her ankles and her hands and barked, "Follow me."

The bottle of water was still on the table where he'd placed it, and that was the only item in the room. She picked it up and followed him.

When he saw her with the water bottle, he laughed and muttered, "Fat chance," then took it away from her.

She didn't say anything. It would have been nice to keep the water bottle, but she wasn't surprised. Men like this were all about control and obedience, making sure she did what he wanted, causing absolutely no trouble for him. That would be the key to surviving this.

He took her to a small bathroom. "You got a couple minutes, and that's it."

She nodded and went inside, grateful when he let her close the door. She went to the bathroom first, her bladder desperate to be emptied, and the relief was huge. She finished, then washed her hands and her face. There was no mirror, but, for that, she was quite grateful. The last thing she wanted was to see what a nightmare she looked like right about now. She opened the door to find him standing in front of it.

He nodded approvingly. "Good, you didn't overdo your stay in there."

She shook her head. "Where's my mother?"

He shrugged. "She's with somebody else, not me."

She didn't say anything to that, and he obviously wouldn't elaborate. She and her mother had been split up for a reason, and Veni knew it was likely all about control again. Her guard led her back to the same room, and, while they'd been gone, somebody else had left behind a blanket and a mattress, a blow-up one perhaps, placed directly on the floor. Regardless she was grateful for any little bit of comfort.

"I'll bring you food in a few minutes."

She nodded and whispered, "Thank you." Then she walked over to the makeshift bed and sat down. She immediately reached for the blanket and pulled it around her, feeling the chill from before hitting her once more. Nothing like coming off the drugs to have your body react with horrible precision in every way you didn't want it to.

He frowned at her. "The food will help."

She didn't say anything, just shut her eyes and sank down into the corner. He closed the door, leaving her alone. As soon as he was gone, she peeked about, careful to not appear to be too excited—in case she was being filmed. She cast a quick glance around to see where she was and if there were any easy way out. She knew the answer would be a hard no, but she had to try. As she searched the windowless room, she was relieved to see no visible signs of any cameras, which also surprised her. However, this room had a high ceiling with rafters, so she suspected any cameras were up there. In a place like this, a prison, cameras would be everywhere.

This looked like maybe another temporary holding position; she wasn't sure. Just enough things about it worried her. She huddled in the cold, waiting for her body to warm up, even as her teeth started to chatter.

When the door opened, and the same guard came inside, he frowned at her, probably when he heard her teeth chattering so badly. "Here's hot soup and some bread." He placed them on the table and stepped back out again. He gave her a searching gaze, as he left.

She didn't care. She knew he would be checking out her reactions, everything she did essentially, and there wouldn't be any easy passes from here on out. Yet she knew that a rescue had to happen. That hope was the only way she and her mother would survive this nightmare. Veni didn't quite know how it would play out, but it would, and she refused to give up on that idea. At least the British government knew they were missing, their rescue plan having gone awry. Now it required a rethink and some time for somebody to come up with something new in order to get them out.

The trouble was her lack of communication, and, at this point, telepathy was seemingly impossible. She could transmit a message, or maybe she could, if and when the rattling in her brain calmed down and the drugs finally eased out of her system. That was the one thing she was hoping for and counting on to get her and her mother out of here.

Surely somebody would be aware that they were missing and would pick up on any signal she sent. At least that was her hope.

The trouble was, right now, every time she sent a signal, it bounced right back. And her skill wasn't the same as a phone signal or something of that nature. So even being deep underground didn't make a difference, at least it never had before. She'd tested it with friends way back when she was in college, when it was all just a big game—until she realized just how dangerous it was and how having this ability was getting her some attention that she didn't want.

Back then she could send messages, even underground, although they weren't of any consequence. She didn't know what, if anything, made a difference now. Somebody could receive them back then too, and *that* might have made the difference. Maybe it wasn't about her ability to send as much as it had been about his ability to receive. And it wasn't the first time she'd thought about Reid in the midst of this nightmare. Or at other times in her life.

She'd wondered about getting his help to secret her out of Russia, but, having no way to contact him, outside of sending telepathic messages, she had held back, just in case somebody else might intercept them. As it was, MI6 had been more than happy to help her and her mother get back to England.

Even now she wondered about Reid. Was he out there? Could she send him a message? Again it might be more about the receiver than the sender. If that were true, he was her best bet. But would he even know what to do or how to contact anybody, assuming he even received her messages? When she finished eating, the door opened, making her suspicious that a camera *was* in this room, just one that she hadn't seen, since the timing was just too damn exact.

She waited until the dish was pulled away, then asked in a low tone, "May I see my mother?"

Immediately came a headshake. "Nope, you no longer have that privilege." And giving that curt response, her guard left and closed the door.

She didn't want to cry, but it was pretty hard not to because she knew that her mother would be suffering even more than Veni was. These guys would make her mother suffer, as punishment for trying to take Veni away from them. That wasn't fair, since Veni wanted to leave, particularly after she'd been coerced into joining up with them in the first place. And, for that, she blamed her father.

Even at that thought, she still didn't know if he was involved. It would break her heart to confirm it, but she wasn't sure there was any other culpable person in her world. Veni's abilities had always bothered her father terribly, and that, in itself, made him one of the most likely people to have been involved in finding her again. Not that she and her mother had told her father what their plans were, so that was a bit of a mystery. Yet somebody had obviously known.

Their workplace may have been bugged, though no plans had ever been made or discussed there. So, when Veni had heard rumors that she would be removed from the area where her mother worked, Veni knew that the time element surrounding their escape would be even more of a crunch. Still, she just couldn't make this change. The news of their taking her away from her mother created a need to speed up their escape plan and to get out of there sooner, which had apparently cost them dearly. Veni found this turn of events to be very hard to live with—until she could find another way out.

And she would find another way out, she vowed. No way she wouldn't. She had to because this was not living. Being forced to work with the Russian government, with whom she didn't agree, a government holding her against her will, was definitely not her thing. Not that anybody here cared.

That was the part that was so hard to understand. She was shocked at how little anybody cared what happened to her, or whether she wanted to do this or not. She had always believed that people had free will, and that was true, until you came up against a government that ensured you didn't, unless your ideas aligned with theirs.

And her kidnapping was too much like her government job. Her day became this unending waiting period, as she anticipated the arrival of her keepers to come back for whatever purpose they had at the time.

Yet it seemed nobody ever came today. She waited and waited, until finally the door opened again, and she was given more food by a different delivery person. She ate quickly, never arguing, never complaining. It didn't matter what it tasted like. It was just food. Once again, she asked the same question. "May I see my mother?"

Another headshake came, and this person left.

Veni knew this guard was more or less just a lackey, somebody to deliver food and to take away food. That was heartbreaking in itself because where were the rest of the people out there, and what were they doing?

Were they all just enjoying watching her squirm and wait, knowing there would be no end to the pain for her because the answers they were giving her were not what she wanted to hear? She closed her eyes yet again and sent out a message to anybody who could hear her. Silent on the ethers, she transmitted an SOS, hoping that somebody would receive her message. She didn't get any response once again, not that she really expected it, but she wouldn't give up hope. Transmissions were like that for her. Sometimes they worked, and sometimes they didn't. She'd never really had a chance to work out the how or the why of her gift, but, given the opportunity now, she would do things very differently.

Finding the limits of what she could do appealed way more than it ever had before. She'd never been in danger before. Now that her captors had changed things to this point of incarceration, she really wanted to know exactly what she could do, when she could do it, and who could help her. Suddenly her complacent, innocent world was not so complacent at all. Although she desperately wanted to find out exactly the same things that the government wanted to find out about her abilities, she didn't want it to be with them, and definitely not when they had plans to utilize it against others.

That would never happen. Yet she didn't know how to stop it because, as long as these people held her and her mother, they would just use her mother against her. And that was something she could never let them do. Hurting her mother wasn't an option, and that meant either Veni had to get herself and her mother out of here fast or she had to find a way to make everybody cooperate, so they didn't hurt her mother. To protect her mother, Veni would have to do what these people wanted, whether Veni liked it or not. The only good thing, as far as she could tell, was that this would not be the final location. Nobody had shown her to a lab or had set any protocols for them to do the testing and the work that these people obviously wanted Veni to do, which meant she would be moved again. And that would be her one and only chance to get out of here—if only she could come up with a plan.

If she were really lucky, she would have somebody to help her and her mother.

REID AND ANDERS sat at a coffee shop, something Reid felt terribly guilty about, while Veni remained in captivity. However, until they had a lead, a direction to go in, they had no choice but to wait. They were going through all the files that they'd been sent by Jonas, and frustration mounted on all sides. Apparently Jonas had already called Terk several times, looking for progress. Of course MI6 was especially anxious to get these two women back. Reid just hoped that MI6 wanted them safe and not just for their own nefarious reasons. Reid didn't have much faith in governments at this point, no matter which one. He looked over at Anders. "Surely, once we get them both to the British government, they will treat them okay, right?"

Anders nodded. "We would like to think so. At least that is the plan. Now, if the UK is on the wrong side of the line, Terk can help them, at least Veni, and Veni will look after her mother. That's what I'm assuming will happen." He frowned at him, saw his frustration. "You're looking really agitated. What's going on?"

Reid nodded. "Yeah, I'm … I'm feeling something, but I can't get a lock on it."

"Is it Veni?" Anders asked, staring at him intently.

"I think so. I think she's trying to send messages, but she seems restricted somehow," he replied. "I don't know whether it's just that or what. I haven't heard from her in a really long time, so I'm having trouble picking up on her signal."

"Okay. I'm not exactly sure how that works, but can you get any kind of location?"

"It feels like it's coming from some distance. It's pretty faint."

"Is that a problem?"

"Generally signals like that don't get faint based on distance," he explained. "So I presume it has to do more with her inability to connect right now, due to some obstruction," he muttered. "I'm getting this weird feeling from …" He stopped, pondered it for a moment, then shrugged and added, "I'll say almost Kazakhstan."

"*Almost* Kazakhstan?" Anders repeated, fascinated.

At that, Reid glared at him. "I get it, and you should know that I don't have any real reason to say it's Kazakhstan over even Germany, but"—he shrugged—"Kazakhstan it is."

"Okay," Anders replied. "I'm willing to go with that. I mean, it's not as if I have any other place to go. Still, I highly doubt going hell-bent for leather off to Kazakhstan, with no direction or particular place to go, will be all that helpful."

"No, probably not," Reid admitted, feeling frustrated. "We need more than just that feeling." Almost immediately his phone rang.

"No, we don't," Terk declared, on the other end. "We're looking at Kazakhstan as a possible location."

"Sure," Reid noted, "but a *possible* location isn't the same thing as an actual destination. If we're seriously going to Kazakhstan, we need to be on the move now because, by the time we get there, they could have moved Veni and her mom again."

"We're trying to get it locked down," Terk explained. "We have somebody close by who might get boots on the ground for us. Levi is hooked into the satellite, getting us some better information. We can get intel out of Kazakhstan, so that's not an issue. Give us twenty minutes."

"We need to be on the move," Reid reminded him, "so twenty minutes is about all you've got."

With that, Terk disconnected.

Reid looked over at Anders, noting his raised eyebrows, and shrugged. "Yes, Terk can read my thoughts even from here. It's fine. Terk and I understand each other, and sometimes he needs to read my mind."

"Apparently," Anders muttered. "So, he agrees with Kazakhstan?"

"He does, but he's waiting on some confirming intel to let us know if it's viable."

Anders looked around the restaurant. "It's pretty hard to accept that, *just because of a feeling*, we'll move multiple countries away on the off-chance that Veni's there, when she was last seen right around the corner of this block."

"I know. But short of us finding anybody who has anything to do with that warehouse and who is still in this part of the world, we might as well start looking ahead, instead of back. Levi's team has already checked the satellite feeds, and nobody has come in or out any of the entrances or exits of either building here in the last couple days."

"Which gives us a big fat lot of nothing." Anders frowned at Reid. "You picked up her energy in that empty warehouse, right?"

"Yes," Reid replied. "I did."

"And that energy doesn't give you anything other than the possibility that she's been here?"

"It gave us that she had definitely been here, but it doesn't give me anything on where she's going. I didn't pick up any of her energy outside of that warehouse."

Anders nodded, his fingers thrumming on the table. They'd both been frustrated, having searched inside the building, plus the back and the front of it, with absolutely nothing popping.

"You know what we need?" Anders suggested. "We need Terk to come up with some information out of Kazakhstan. Surely they've got some contacts."

"It sounded like that's what they were working on," Reid reminded him.

"Maybe, but it seems we should have some contacts there too." He pulled out his phone and started texting.

"Who're you texting?" Reid asked cautiously.

"Levi, just to see if they have anyone over there because, if that's where we think Veni is, she's way too close to Russia, to her final destination, and we need to get there fast."

"Which is something we need to do now." Reid stood up.

At that, Anders eyed him. "You got a way to get us there?"

"No, but we'll get one pretty quickly lined up," he muttered. "We have to. Her time is running out. Once she gets into the Eastern Bloc, we'll have a hell of a time getting her out of there."

"Hey, Kazakhstan will already cause us some trouble," he muttered.

Reid gave him a ghost of a smile. "That's true, but we can get in and out of there in a heartbeat, and nobody, literally nobody, will be the wiser. But once we start hitting the Russian borders? … That's kind of the Wild West."

Anders finished sending the text to Levi, then got up and walked over to the counter, where he changed their orders to take-out. While he waited, he picked up an assortment of snacks from the front counter.

By the time he was done over there, Reid had locked down their transport, then joined Anders and said, "Let's go."

"Yeah? How're we traveling?"

"It'll be a little bit different," he replied hesitantly, looking over at him. "I understand you fly helicopters, right?"

"I have a license," he clarified. "I've been working on it at Levi's place. One of the things I plan to do is stay and be a replacement pilot."

"Not a bad idea," he muttered. "Anyway, we're flying by helicopter from a small landing strip nearby, and apparently Jonas set us up with a trip into Kazakhstan. Not sure what we'll owe MI6 for this though, or what Veni will want."

"That's tomorrow's issue," Anders said. "I wonder if MI6 can get us in without raising any alarms, considering they already lost their people."

"Not only did they lose Veni and her mother, they also lost their own team members," he reminded him.

"It's a constant reminder of the world we live in," Anders noted. "Let's get going. We don't have much time to sit and debate the merits of MI6."

And, with that, a hired car pulled right up in front of the café. They hopped inside, headed to a small helipad, owned by a private corporation. They were airborne within minutes, and, just under an hour later, they landed, quickly boarded a private plane, and were airborne again.

At the smooth moves and shifts, Anders smiled. "Sure glad some people can organize transports like this," he stated, with a laugh. "It's frustrating when you have to spend too much time waiting on commercial travel."

"We don't have the time or the inclination for commercial travel," Reid commented. "I mean, as far as I can tell, we've got …" Then he hesitated, unsure of whether to say it or not.

"We've got what?" Anders asked him. "If you know something, you need to tell me."

"It's not that I know something. All I can do is tell you that something out there is coming toward us, that's not very fun."

"It never is," he conceded. "I would still rather know ahead of time, than after the fact, even if I don't know the details."

"Got it. I'm just getting this horrible pressure, and I don't know whether it's her mother or Veni, but I think she's sending messages, and I think she's sending them almost in a panic."

"Yes, but how else would she send messages?" Anders asked.

His calm reasoning, critical thinking, and accepting nature was something Reid appreciated. "If she were running an experiment, or if she were calm, then her messages would go out at a much greater distance and much quicker. She's quite a strong transmitter, but she's not trained, and that could be hindering her right now."

"When you say, *not trained*—"

"Meaning that she's never put any time or effort into seeing what she could do. Back when I knew her, it was little more than a joke to her. Yet she is very powerful. I told her that she should look into it, but she just laughed and said it was a one-off, not for her. I suspect she meant that, right up until it came down to something happening to her mother. At that point in time, all bets were off."

"If you think about it, that makes a lot of sense. Veni didn't see any value in developing her skills, having no logical pathway ahead of her. So she probably couldn't see any point in pursuing it."

"Exactly. I think that's spot on. She was also starting to work with her mother in microbiology and potentially put it to use there."

"Whoa, whoa, whoa," Anders replied, turning to look at him. "How the hell do you put a gifted transmitter to work in some science or medical lab?"

He gave his partner a ghost of a smile. "She was doing stem cell work, regenerative stem cells, and that is all about sending signals."

Anders blinked several times. "Hang on a minute. Are you telling me there's a scientific application for telepathy?"

"It's possible, but I don't know. Maybe I'm out to lunch," Reid said. "I haven't talked to her and don't know anything about it. However, it occurred to me that somebody who can send signals in a very different way may very well generate interest from a government that is working hard on cutting-edge stem cell research. There are people in a race all over the world," he explained, "looking for a way to live forever and all that, and a lot of people think the key to that is coming from stem cells. In particular, if you can get specific stem cells to regenerate or to turn back the clock, which is definitely not my expertise, or cup of tea," he admitted, "then you think about something or *somebody* who can send signals, potentially at a deeper level than done before. That scenario could be a recipe for disaster for Veni, yet a recipe for incredible success for the government involved."

"Sounds like a nightmare," Anders muttered. "Whatever happened to growing old gracefully? I was kind of looking forward to it."

Reid burst out laughing. "You just might get that wish. Then again, by the time you get old, there could be half-a-dozen different alternatives to dying."

"I don't know about that," he countered. "Sometimes I think we're meant to grow old and die, then regenerate. That's the whole purpose behind life," he stated. "Living forever, if you're young and healthy, is one thing, but living forever when you're already eighty or ninety with various troubles, pains, and broken-down bodies doesn't exactly appeal."

"If you want to live forever, then in theory you should live and enjoy the perks of life in a clean, healthy body. But we're not even close to there yet, and, no, I don't know any of the details. I'm just someone who's kind of fascinated with the process."

"Seems that Veni's mother is too."

"It's the kind of work she was doing, and, if her mother had any idea that this was something that Veni could do, I can see her mother dragging Veni on board to help out. I've got mixed feelings as to whether we should be messing with genetics, though."

Anders nodded. "I'm not sure I'm a believer in that either."

"Doesn't matter whether we are or not because, if Veni can pull off this stem cell magic, then both mother and daughter are lost to us, and we'll never get them free. Not only do the Russians want that kind of information for themselves, they also don't want the US or the UK or any other country to get that kind of an edge over them."

They quickly switched to another plane for the next leg of their journey, and, once they were seated, Anders looked over at him. "I'll crash until we arrive. Wake me up in time, will you?"

Reid nodded, working on his phone.

As Anders got comfortable, he asked, "What will you do?"

"I'll send some telepathic messages to Veni. The tone of what she is sending has changed," he shared. "I'll see if she can receive anything."

"I thought you told me how she wasn't a receiver."

He looked over at him, then smiled. "She's not."

Anders stared at him for a moment. "Do I want to know how you'll do this?"

"Probably not," he replied, with a big grin. "Doesn't mean it'll work, but sometimes, … especially when people are frazzled, worried, and panicked even, you can get in through kind of a back door in their brain that allows you to subdue them, to calm them down, and to let them know they're not alone."

"If that were possible, don't you think Terk would have done it by now?"

"Maybe, but he hasn't been monitoring how panicked

she's been. She's getting worse, which means, for whatever reason, either they're moving her, and she realizes that her chances of getting out of this are now almost impossible, or it's got something to do with her mother."

"I presume they're keeping her mother separate from Veni. Although, if what you say is true, they need both the mother and the daughter, and they need them together in order to make this work."

"Exactly, and that will also mean they need an agreement from both. However, in order to get it, their captors won't really care about their methodology."

# CHAPTER 4

NO MATTER HOW many times Veni asked, the answer was always the same. She couldn't see her mother. She was afraid her mother may not be alive anymore. She wasn't in the greatest health to begin with, and, with all the drugs she'd been dosed with throughout this kidnapping, quite heavily too, it was possible they'd caused a problem for her mother. For that, Veni would never forgive them, but she was a long way from making them pay, and that was something else that drove her crazy.

When the door opened the next time, she was half dozing. Startled, she stared up at the man, a stranger.

He looked around several times, then frowned at her. "Hardly the nicest accommodations."

She shrugged. "I highly doubt anybody here cares."

He nodded. "Of course you would believe that, but we're really not animals."

She studied him warily. The friendly approach always came with a more conditioning strategy, and she wasn't really up for any of those.

"I hear from my men that you're asking to see your mother."

She nodded. "Yes, she was kidnapped with me."

"Kidnapped?" he repeated, opening his eyes wide. "That's rather strong terminology."

"Not at all," she stated carefully. "It is what it is."

He glared at her.

She didn't say anything more, knowing that this would be the one man she would have to watch out for. He might be playing the game and projecting himself to be a nice guy at the moment, but absolutely no way behind that facade did he give a crap about anything but what he had come for. Naturally she wasn't buying it and was highly suspicious.

"The good news is your mother is alive, and she's asking about you."

Veni felt instantaneous relief, even though she tried hard not to let him see it, but, of course, he did.

He smiled. "See? We're really not so bad."

She didn't say anything.

"And now I suppose you'll want to see her," he added, with an almost disinterested shrug. "Of course, in order to let you see her, I'll need something."

"What do you want?" she asked warily.

He smiled. "For one thing, we're not at all happy that you tried to leave us in the first place," he shared. "Everybody was pretty sure they were treating you right, and we had no reason to believe that you weren't a very welcome and wanted member of the scientific community here."

She just stared at him because, if anything was further from the truth, she'd yet to hear it. She had been a prisoner, so the comment was hardly worth responding to.

"Apparently you didn't see it that way. Otherwise I don't know why you would have chosen to try to leave."

"If any of that was true, then leaving wasn't something I would have had to try. Leaving would have been something I was entitled to do."

"We don't really like it when people leave, especially

when we're busy doing extremely sensitive research," he explained, looking at her. "We just want your cooperation."

She stared at him, not sure what she was supposed to say to that, knowing that he sought a whole lot more than cooperation.

He nodded. "You don't like that either, I see. You're really not a team player, are you?" he asked, with a small smile.

"I'm not a team player at all, when I'm a kidnap victim by force," she stated calmly. "There is nothing else to call this, when I am a victim of whatever shenanigans you guys are up to."

"Shenanigans," he repeated, with a smile. "I like that. It's a great term. Now, obviously you aren't terribly impressed, but that's okay. We're hoping that this next stay will make you a little more cooperative."

Her heart sank at that because it just meant they would make her life a lot more miserable.

"We will be moving you soon, but not today. Your mother is not in the best of health." He enunciated every word.

It was so hard to not respond.

"She really wants to see you, but, if you won't cooperate, well, … obviously you won't get to see her." And, with that, he nodded. "I think I'll have a hot cup of tea." As he walked to the door, he stopped and looked back at her. "Think about it."

Both the tea reference and the mention of her mother's ill health were just more games. Obviously Veni would love a cup of tea, but, since that wasn't even being offered, he was using it as a reminder of all the things that she wouldn't get, quite likely ever again, all because Veni had rejected their little rules and had tried to walk away from them. Being a prisoner was one thing, but being a prisoner like that? No, not her style. Not anybody's style, and maybe that was the problem.

As she thought back to the other people who were there at the lab, she wondered whether one of them had noticed a change in Veni's behavior or had in some way lied to get her in trouble. And it had coincidentally occurred with such perfect timing that they were on their way out the door … and out of the country. Even now, Veni was tired of traveling, but, hey, she would take as many trips as it would take, if it would get her out of this mess.

As she sat, her head bowed on her forearms, fervently hoping that her mother was okay, Veni felt something, like a weird tapping in her mind. She stiffened and looked around cautiously, still not sure if anybody was watching her because rafters were up above, and it always reminded her of the possibility that cameras could be pointed down at her. She didn't know what espionage equipment looked like these days, but she knew it must have advanced considerably, probably well beyond anything she could ever dream up. Again, the tapping came, a steady *tap-tap-tap*. She frowned and, in her mind, whispered, *Hello?*

There was more tapping and still more, as if somebody was there, but they weren't getting the message. Then again, she was a transmitter. That didn't mean the person on the other end was a receiver. She could just hope that somebody out there had an idea that she was in all this trouble. When the tapping continued, she glared all around her, only to realize again that someone could be watching her. She immediately subsided, but, confirming her suspicion, the door opened, and somebody stepped in and did a quick search of the place. Not seeing anything, he turned, then glared at her and walked out.

If she'd ever needed a second confirmation that she was being watched, that was it. And it sucked because that also meant they were watching her when she slept. They were watching her, seeing if she had any contact with anyone, not that she had, but it was a reminder that she needed to be even more careful.

Just then, the tapping resumed. Keeping her face blank, she closed her eyes and pulled the blanket up around her face, as if to go to sleep, then immediately started sending messages. *Who are you? Who are you? Who are you? Who are you?*

Just when she thought maybe somebody was getting through to her, with the tempo of taps stopping and starting again, then the tapping stopped completely. Frowning, she shifted uneasily, feeling pain in her heart, like she hadn't felt in a long time. Worried for her mother and now wondering if the stupid food she'd eaten was drugged, she felt herself slowly succumbing to a deep sleep once again.

"DAMMIT," REID MUTTERED.

Anders stretched, waking up slowly to look at him. "I presume you're still trying to contact her."

"I thought I was getting somewhere," he shared. "There was a weird connection, or at least I thought there was. She seemed to be sending an SOS, and I was trying to reassure her that we were here. I was hoping to get her to connect, but nothing came, and now it's just … she's gone offline again."

"*Offline, … connect,*" Anders repeated, shaking his head. "I don't speak the language, I guess."

"Yes, there is a specific jargon," he confirmed, with a smile. "But it's not all that different from anything else electronic that we have. Think about your cell phone battery dying."

"Does she have a battery like that?"

"We all have batteries to a certain extent. Terk's recharges on the go, and mine is pretty good at staying charged. I need sleep to recharge. That's usually the biggest thing for me. In Veni's case, I'm not sure what she needs to do. Right now she's not sending or receiving in any way," Reid described. "It's all just blank."

"Sleeping or even drugged maybe?" Anders asked.

"Could be. My guess is, if she's getting weaker, it could be either one," Reid replied. "Although, if they'll move her again, I suspect the easiest way would be keeping her isolated and drugged."

"They must really be afraid of her."

"I suspect they are," Reid noted. "I'm not kidding when I say she was a really strong transmitter."

"But what good is a transmitter if you don't have a receiver?"

"That's what her point has always been." He gave Anders a crooked smile. "At the time, she didn't particularly like a suggestion I made and pretty much got in my face for it."

"What suggestion was that?" Anders asked, looking over at him, as he stretched again.

"I simply told her that I happen to be a receiver."

Anders started to laugh. "Of course you are. How did I not guess that?"

"Hey, we were good friends, and I really liked her, but she had made it abundantly clear that she was destined for other things."

"Yeah, I wonder how she feels about that right about now."

"Don't know," Reid muttered, "and it's not as if I have a chance to ask her."

"Hold that thought," Anders declared. "With any luck we'll get through this, and you can ask her yourself."

"Yeah, well, I suspect she's still probably not too interested in anything I have to offer."

"Oh, I wouldn't count on that," Anders argued. "You're perfectly positioned to be the hero who comes and rescues her. That could go a long way toward clearing up all kinds of things."

"Maybe so, but who wants a relationship based on that?"

"Once you have a relationship, you can build it into something else, but you have to get your foot in the door first. From the sounds of things, she pretty well slammed it on you the last time."

"Yep, she sure did," Reid agreed. "Can't say I'm too interested in revisiting that chapter."

"I wonder about that," Anders countered, but his tone was dry, with almost a silent humor.

Reid looked at him, with an eyebrow raised. "Meaning?"

"Meaning that Levi has this tendency to pair people up. I know everybody at Terk's place has fallen madly in love too, so maybe Levi's and Terk's whole love magic thing is continuing and spreading somewhere else now."

"Yeah, I heard about that," Reid stated, "though I can't say I've ever experienced any of that magic myself."

"No, me either, but then this is your job right now,"

Anders pointed out. "I'm completely out of it, since I'm already well and truly hitched," Anders noted, with a big smile. "That is something I wouldn't change for the world. But you, on the other hand, still have a long way to go."

"*Great.*" Reid rolled his eyes. "I appreciate the way you put that."

Anders laughed. "How long until we land?"

"Twenty minutes, and then we have to pick up a rental. Beyond that point, we're on our own."

"Got it," Anders said. "That's the way I prefer to hunt."

"Me too," Reid agreed. "We're still waiting for Terk to come up with some intel as to where we're going though."

At that, Anders looked at him, startled. "Nobody's gotten back to us on that?"

"Nope, not yet," Reid stated, "and that's where the concern is. We're not exactly sure where she is, and we don't have a target area to start looking."

"Kazakhstan isn't exactly a small place," Anders muttered. "An awful lot is going on in that country too."

"Exactly, and if we talk to the wrong people—"

Anders nodded. "We're screwed. Tell me again why we're even here?'

"Because of me," Reid declared, with a wry look. "Sorry about that."

"It's fine, but don't you have anybody on staff who can sort out where Veni is?"

"They've been using all the usual methods to no avail. But a guy on Terk's team—a relative newcomer, I guess—is apparently a locator, specifically, a direction finder. Don't ask me what that is because I've never worked with one before."

Anders looked at him in surprise. "I think I remember

hearing something about that on another case," he muttered. "The guy can only give you directions, like literally *go left* or whatever, but, hey, maybe that's all we need."

"I don't know. It still sounds kind of dodgy."

Anders started to laugh. "Isn't that my line? This is all pretty dodgy, if you ask me, and I feel kind of useless to tell you the truth."

"Not at all. You'll still get to do it your way, but, in this kind of scenario, we have a little bit more of a helping hand. And I hate to admit it, but, all too often, that helping hand turns out to be completely useless."

Anders nodded. "Yeah, there have definitely been times where we could have used a helping hand, and it wasn't there or available," he shared. "Not that we blame people with your gifts, by any means. There's always an understanding that, when it's there, it's gold, and, when it's not, well, back to the drawing board and the good old-fashioned ways we've always done things."

"Exactly, and that's the way we'll work this one. If our direction finder can help us sort out who, where, what, and how, that's even better, but there's a good chance he'll be just as lost as we are."

"Time will tell, and we'll know soon enough."

Just then the plane started to descend. "Can't say I'll be upset to get out of these airplanes and on the ground again," Reid admitted. "Just something about traveling this way makes me feel as if everything is out of control. I really would prefer to be behind the wheel."

"You and me both," Anders said, as they buckled up for the landing. "What we need now is that little bit of intel to shake something loose."

"When we land, we'll check in and see if they've come

up with anything. It can't be complete silence."

"If it is, and the kidnappers are planning on moving her again, it will be almost impossible to find her and her mother."

Reid nodded. "I know, and that's why I'm not even considering it."

With that, they settled back and waited for the plane to land. Before long they were in their rental and on the road. Anders drove, as Reid spoke to Terk on the phone.

"Okay, we're heading to the city, but we have no idea where we're going."

"I've got Langdon here, trying to sort it out, but he's not really picking up anything," Terk shared apologetically.

"Fine, I get that. Unfortunately we get that all too often, but we still need some idea of where Veni is."

"Yeah, unless you want to start the old-fashioned way, taking her picture around."

"We'll have to, but it would sure as hell help if we had the right city at least."

Terk laughed. "We're pretty sure that you've got the right city, so don't double-check yourself on that. Once we get any better directions, I'll let you know."

Reid ended the call with a groan and looked over at Anders. "So far they don't have squat. We're here, and, yet, if I'm wrong, it's a completely wasted trip."

"So, let's not go on the assumption that you're wrong," Anders pointed out. "You were pretty adamant about it at the time."

"Yeah, and nothing like time to make you wonder if you were a fool," he admitted, staring out at the scenery all around them. Just then he got a text. "*Huh.*"

"Yeah, and what's that text about?" Anders asked.

"Langdon says, *go left*."

Anders looked at him in surprise. They were on a multilane highway, with multiple vehicles all around them. "Yeah, and whereabouts does he want me to go left?"

It came back in all caps. **LEFT NOW!**

Immediately Anders changed lanes, swearing at the lack of details in the text and the last-minute timing. By the time they'd navigated into the leftmost lane and hit the exit, he looked over at Reid and muttered, "Please tell me this guy's got something good."

"I have no idea." Reid stared at his phone, as if a viper were about to strike again. "All I got was *left* and then *left now*."

"Yeah, I got that much," Anders stated, "and here we are, *left*, meaning *left now*, but where the hell is that leading us to?"

As Reid looked up and around, he noted they were heading into a suburban area, with marginally maintained structures and farmhouses with big fields but not big orchards. It was more like small farms that people were using for housing, more than working farms. "I'm not exactly sure where we are, but that was a pretty specific order." Just then his phone buzzed again. He looked down and muttered, "At the next light, … on the next corner"—waiting for each message to come in—"turn left."

At that, Anders looked over at him in surprise. "Seriously?"

He nodded. "All I can tell you is what this text says, and it's not as if we have anything else to go on, so we might as well."

Shaking his head, Anders followed the directions.

Reid noted the small lane that Anders drove along, with

big farmhouses on either side, but again they were in a poorer area, and these were definitely locals, not farmers. A few people stared at them as they drove by, suspicion on their faces, no sign of a warm welcome. "It definitely isn't a place that a stranger will be welcome," Reid stated.

His phone buzzed again. With an eye roll, Reid quickly read it out loud. "Left and then the next left." Then came another message.

**Sorry, I don't know where this will take you, but that's all I've got for now.**

Frowning, Reid read the latest text to Anders, as they took the first left, then almost immediately a second left. Then they pulled into a driveway. "Shit."

Immediately an old man stepped out, glaring at them.

Reid muttered, "He doesn't know why we're here, and neither do I, but this is all we've got."

"Well, crap," Anders replied, as the old man came toward them, with fury on his face. "You know we're not welcome here, right?"

"Yeah, we aren't. But the question is why, and does it have anything to do with the missing women?"

# CHAPTER 5

A HAND GENTLY stroked her cheek, then pinched her neck gently. Veni winced and tried to pull away.

"Don't," a woman said. "We don't have much time."

Veni opened her eyes slowly to see her mother staring at her. It took a moment to understand just how unusual this was. Then they enveloped each other in a tight emotional hug.

Her mother was crying, yet trying to talk through her tears, as she whispered, "We don't have much time."

Veni frowned at her. "Time for what?"

"I've managed to buy us a few moments together," she murmured, "but they won't have patience for long."

"What do they want?"

"They want us to go back, of course," she whispered, with a sigh. "Plus they want us to stay there and cooperate and never try this again."

Veni winced at that. "Are they listening to us right now?"

Her mother's tone lowered, as she whispered, "I would imagine so."

Veni looked around, and their guard was leaning against the door, watching the two of them. She couldn't stop hugging her mother, as she whispered, "Are you okay? Did they hurt you?"

"No, they didn't. I'm fine," she replied. "You?"

She nodded. "I'm fine too. Of course we know that is only a temporary circumstance, unless we agree to cooperate."

"Exactly."

She glanced at the guard, who even now was looking around nervously. "Nobody knows?"

"No, I had to bribe him."

"Of course. At least that's one thing you can count on over here. Yet you took a big risk," Veni replied, "and, if he gets in trouble, he'll ensure that you pay."

"I know, but I need to know if there's anything ..." Then she stopped.

"Anything I can do?"

"I needed to know that you were okay regardless."

"I'm fine," she whispered. She held her mom tight, and, into her hair, she whispered, "I can't seem to communicate with anyone. Something's wrong."

Her mother stiffened, and then her shoulders sagged, as she nodded. "The drugs."

"I don't know. I'm ... I'm still trying. I was hoping that maybe somebody could find us, if we could leave something behind."

Her mother stiffened at that, wondering if that were even possible. "I ... I'm just grasping at straws here. ... I'm feeling a little on the desperate side now."

"You and me both," Veni muttered. "I'm working on it, and I'll keep trying."

"Remember that you can do way more than you ever thought you could. We've proven that time and time again."

"Maybe, but these aren't the best conditions to try something like that."

"It doesn't matter," her mom said. "Circumstances like this show you who you really are." She struggled to meet her gaze, then pleaded, "Can't you reach out to people you've known in the past?"

"I've tried," Veni stated. "One guy I used to play these games with all the time. I've reached out to him, but I'm not … Remember? I'm a transmitter, as they call it, and I am not a receiver."

"Yet surely that has to be two halves of the same thing."

Veni waved a hand, still keeping her tone low, as she held her mom close. "I understand, yet that isn't the easiest thing to change on the spur of the moment."

"No." Her mom pulled back, hearing the guard, as she looked down at her daughter. "Still, times like this bring out the best in us, and, when we insist on change, it often shows up because we need it to," she murmured.

Just then, the guard hissed.

She immediately got to her feet and looked down on her daughter with a teary smile. "Stay safe." And, with that, she walked over to the guard, who quickly led her away.

Absolutely over the moon, having seen her mom and knowing she was doing okay, Veni now had to turn her attention to figuring out how to get out of here. Her mind had possibly been impacted by the drugs, plus her fear for her mother had rendered Veni less proactive as well. That was something she wouldn't allow to last much longer.

The door closed, and she sank back down. Was anybody watching at this very moment? She wouldn't take any chances. She closed her eyes, wrapped herself up tight in the blanket, and started sending a message, as strong and clear as she could, about how she needed help, that they needed help. Damned being just a transmitter. If she would be *just* a transmitter, she would be the best damn transmitter she could be. And not for the first time in her life, she cursed her decision to *not* develop these abilities, having not seen any future in it. Yet now, all she could see were the advantages of having something like this available to her.

It would help a lot if she had somebody to send the messages to, and the only one she could really reach out to was Reid. Dammit, if he was out there and if he was getting some messages, all the better because maybe he would have the ability to contact somebody and get the word out that they were in trouble.

With that thought in mind, she kept sending as many messages as hard as she could. When she fatigued, she closed her eyes and did it again and then again and again. When a tone slammed into her brain, she froze, looking around wildly, trying to figure out just what she had heard. Yet the door to her room was closed, and nobody was in here with her. Unfortunately her mother hadn't returned, and even now Veni still had no idea what was going on. But she had surely heard someone.

When that tone slammed in her head again, she froze.

*Message received.*

Wild and terrified, she looked around, then whispered to the ethers, *Seriously?*

It came back again. *Yes, seriously.*

She let out a slow breath. *Who are you?*

*Somebody who can help*, the man replied.

She froze at that. *Who are you?* she asked, bolting to her feet and looking around cautiously.

*A friend* came the same tone. *People are looking for you. Can you give us any location as to where you are?*

That was the next problem. Now that she had contacted

somebody, and, God help her, she didn't know how that worked and didn't even know who this person was or how they knew she had reached out to Reid. Now she was afraid she had opened up a pathway to somebody who would betray her because that's what these people did. This was what they wanted from her, a display of her abilities. Had she just unwittingly fallen into their trap? But the calm tone was still there, still waiting for an answer. She whispered cautiously, *No, I can't.*

*Good enough*, he replied. *Are you both in decent health?*

*Yes*, she answered again cautiously, wondering whether this was just another test and a trap.

Then in a soothing tone, he added, *Stay open. I'll be back.* And, with that, he was gone.

She wanted to cry out for him to come back. The contact with somebody, anybody from the outside world, had risen an unbelievably strong hope within her. Yet what was she supposed to do when there was absolutely nobody here to talk to? Maybe she was just going crazy, and she'd imagined it all. And worse, maybe it was the Russians, who were now over the moon, since Veni had finally reached out, and they had the proof they were looking for on what she could and couldn't do, something she'd been desperate to hide from them. And yet she'd willingly opened up and told somebody else, some stranger, that she was here. What had she done?

Horrified, she sank back onto the mattress, staring around her, wondering how she could reverse what she'd just done, when the door opened, and one of the guards stepped in, walked around the room, and stared at her with an odd look, before walking away again. That just reminded her that she had to be more careful. She'd bolted to her feet in shock, and now they were in here, looking around to see what she'd seen.

That would surely bring other people in as well, to see what her problem was, to see if she was communicating with anybody. Chances were good they would just knock her out with drugs again, rendering her unable to do anything. And, if this unknown person talking in her head was there to help, it wouldn't make any difference because Veni couldn't respond, not once they pumped her full of drugs again.

The door opened again, and two men stepped in, one with a long needle. With tears in her eyes, in a last-ditch effort, she sent a hard message to Reid.

*Being drugged and pulled back under. Please find me.*

And, with that, she lost consciousness.

REID STARED AT the old man screaming at them at the top of his lungs in a language that they didn't understand, and he wasn't even giving them a chance to say anything. The old man acted as if they had slighted him in some way. When someone shouted at him, the angry old man turned and glared, but his demeanor changed at the appearance of the second man. The old guy shot another look at Reid and Anders, then turned and went back into his house.

The second man—in some sort of uniform but one Reid didn't recognize—walked toward them, his tone guttural as he spoke. "You really set him off."

They shrugged at that. "Sorry, we just pulled into his driveway, and he came out running."

The other man gave a half smile. "He doesn't take kindly to strangers."

"Did I hear something about his car being stolen?'

The other man nodded. "Yes, it was taken a few days ago. That's another reason why he went off on you," he replied. "Sorry, unless, of course, you guys took it."

"No, but we're interested in who might have."

"Why?" he asked. "What are you even doing here?" He looked at them suspiciously.

Reid smiled. "We're looking to find two women who were kidnapped."

At that, the other man's eyebrows shot up. "Around here? That's strange. I haven't heard of any women missing around here."

"No, but they were brought here," Reid clarified, infusing his tone with confidence to confirm the information that he had received energetically with actual fact. Of course they were a long way from having that fact in their heads.

The other man shook his head. "Of course you don't know from where."

"Right. No, we don't, but it brought us here."

"Good luck with that," he said, with a note of humor. "This old guy can't stand anybody, and the last thing he would have done is kidnap two women."

Reid glanced at Anders, as he asked the newcomer, "What about his vehicle?"

With that question, a curious look crossed the other man's face. "Now that's an interesting idea. We really don't get much theft around here, and his vehicle went missing a few days ago."

"No sign of it since?"

"No, no sign of it since, which is why everybody is quite pissed off about the whole thing."

"Of course," Reid agreed. "And we're not here to upset

him any further."

"Too late for that," the stranger noted, with a chuckle, "because you've definitely upset him. Yet he upsets easily. Now, if you were to return his vehicle, that would be a whole different story."

"That might not be possible, but it's certainly something we would give consideration to, if we had the chance. What can you tell us about it?"

"It's a small white car. He left it out, as we always leave our vehicles out. However, he'd just had it tuned up, and it was sitting outside, still running because he'd had some problems with the battery. He had planned to take it back to the mechanic and yell and scream at him over that problem. Instead it was stolen, and he thinks the mechanic took it."

"Ah, right, and I suppose that's possible too, isn't it?"

"Everything is possible," he murmured.

"Don't suppose you know what the license plate is, do you?"

He looked surprised, but then he nodded. "I do because we were out looking for it to see if it showed up somewhere." He provided them with the license plate number. "If you find it, I'm sure the old man will talk to you."

"If it's linked to our case, we'll do our best," Reid replied.

"And if it's not?"

"If we come across it, we'll definitely let you know. Vehicles are stolen on a regular basis, it seems."

"Yes, but not around here, not very often anyway," the stranger added. "We're a small town, and nobody cares much. You wouldn't even be here yourselves, if you weren't looking for somebody."

"And the people we're after wouldn't have come here

unless they thought it was a good place where they could hide these women."

At that, the other man nodded, with a shrug of acknowledgment. "That's a good point that I hadn't considered. Lots of properties are out in the back hills. I personally haven't seen any newcomers to the area, but, if these women are prisoners, I wouldn't have, would I?" Then he slid a gaze over the men.

"No, you wouldn't have," Reid agreed, with a nod. "Chances are, they're being kept hidden. And it looks as if there are lots of places around here to do that."

He shrugged. "My heart goes out to them. Playing games like that isn't fair to anyone," he muttered. "And who kidnaps women? I've never understood that sort of thing." At that, he looked around and added, "If you find the car, let us know, and if you don't, well, that's just the way life goes."

"Was it insured?"

He looked back at him and shook his head. "He doesn't do insurance."

Reid winced. "Ouch, that makes it harder."

"It absolutely does, but we can tell people until we're blue in the face about things like insurance, but it doesn't seem to change anything."

"No, it won't, especially if insurance is yet another cost that most people here can't afford."

"Exactly. Thank you." And, with that, the guy nodded. "I'll wait here until you leave."

Reid and Anders shared a glance, then shrugged and got back into their vehicle.

As they pulled out of the driveway, Anders asked, "You want to tell me what that stop was all about?"

"Not sure I can," Reid admitted cheerfully. "That lead

was based on information that came from Langdon, the locator."

"Right," Anders replied, "all that *turn left* business."

"And yet it pulled us into a property where their vehicle had been stolen recently. I'm passing that information along to the team."

It didn't take more than ten minutes of their driving through town, trying to get a lay of the land, before Terk called Reid back. He answered and put the call on Speaker.

"That's an interesting vehicle," Terk shared.

"Why?"

"Because, according to a police account, it was found in a ditch not too far from that address."

"Yet they didn't contact the owner?"

"It's apparently in pretty rough shape, and they were thinking that maybe the owner perished in the accident. Honestly the process over there isn't very fast or very efficient."

"So, what then? They found the vehicle, but it was to-taled?"

"Yes, per the local authorities, but it was stolen, according to you."

"Correct," Reid confirmed. "I was hoping that maybe somebody had decided they might need that vehicle to move the two women. Any chance we can look at it?"

"I would suggest you do just that. It's in a junkyard right now, since deemed as totaled, and no way the owner will get it back. Plus it's not drivable, so there is that."

"Right, I wonder if he already knew about all that."

"That would imply that the other man you spoke to knew about this as well."

"Yeah, well, interesting how quickly he was on the scene." He turned to look over at Anders, who was listening in. "And also odd how quickly the old man immediately shut down his yelling and screaming, once he saw this other guy."

"Right, so maybe his vehicle is something they already know about, and the other man wondered if you guys had taken it or not."

"That's possible, or he didn't care if we had taken it or not, and we were just another likely target. Definitely something weird is going on in this town."

"Something weird is going on in every town," Anders noted, with a wry look. "People don't like strangers and don't like people interfering."

"Maybe. I'll keep you updated, Terk."

As he put away his phone, he leaned forward, only to have something slam hard inside his head. He sat back, gasping, his body shuddering with the force.

Anders quickly pulled off to the side of the road. "Dude, what's wrong?"

"I'm not sure," he muttered, holding his head with both hands. "Good God, my head's just booming."

"And booming isn't good, I gather."

Reid frowned at him blankly for a moment. "Could it be somebody trying to contact me?"

"You tell me," Anders quipped, studying him, with one eyebrow up. "This is one of the strangest missions I've ever been on."

"While I try to figure this out," he muttered, still gasping with pain, "why don't you try to figure out what you would do, if you didn't have me and Terk and Langdon along for the ride."

"I *don't* have them along for the ride," he replied in a dry tone. "I'm not sure just what all Terk and Langdon have picked up in this corner of the world either, but it doesn't mean it has anything to do with our case."

The pounding in Reid's head increased, then, all of a sudden, a message was emblazoned in his head.

*Help! I need help!*

He straightened and turned to look at Anders. "It's Veni," he cried out. "She's sending a message for help."

Anders nodded, as he turned the vehicle back onto the road. "Let's hope she can tell us something this time."

"No, she can't. At least not yet."

"Of course not." He shook his head. "I'm beginning to think you guys are hindered by these abilities because, so far, I haven't seen that it's of any value against someone who knows what you can do."

"Not yet maybe, but stick around," Reid stated, wanting to smile. Yet the pain and the immense amount of energy slamming into his brain was intense. "I'm not sure what's going on, but wow."

"Can you get a location? Can you get anything?'

"I'm a receiver. I can receive whatever she's sending. She's a transmitter, but she's only sending that she needs help."

"Again, not helpful," Anders muttered, as he headed down to the far end of town and the junkyard.

# CHAPTER 6

VENI OPENED HER eyes to find her door to her temporary prison opening again. She waited, hoping against hope that it would be her mother, but of course not.

The jailer who had threatened her earlier, stepped in, and smiled at her. "So, any more cooperation out of you?"

She stared at him in surprise. "Cooperation?" she asked carefully. "Like what?"

He stared at her. "Here I was nice enough to let your mother come in and see you." She didn't say anything to that and just waited. "So, since I did something nice for you, you can do something nice for me."

"Like what?" she repeated.

"Tell me who you were talking to."

Her eyebrows shot up, and her heart sank. "What do you mean?"

He sighed. "See? That's the problem I'm having right now. I went out of my way to ensure you got something you really wanted. Now, I want something, and you're not giving it to me."

"I don't know what you're trying to tell me," she replied. "If I could cooperate, I would."

"No, you wouldn't, but, according to my jailer, you started acting irrationally, as if you were talking to somebody."

She stared at him in surprise, and then relief washed over her face deliberately, as she nodded. "Yes, I was talking to me. I was trying to give myself a pep talk, so, yeah. … I presume I *was* acting irrationally," she shared, with a nod.

He stared at her for a long moment. "I did see the video."

"Okay, and doesn't that fit?" she asked in surprise. "Or are you saying I was sleepwalking?"

He frowned, then looked back to the hallway outside her room, where she was being held. "I'll take another look." And, with that, he disappeared.

She sank back against the wall and closed her eyes, deliberately keeping her face schooled, knowing that he would likely be back soon, if her explanation didn't satisfy him. He was looking for more, but she didn't have more to give, and she didn't dare. The thought of getting out of here alive kept her going, and to give her kidnappers any confirmation of her skills would just make her life even more difficult.

Once they found out that she could do something unique, it would bring a much greater hardship, even compared to her current hardships, on both her and her mom. The fact remained that Veni couldn't even do very much on the *special* spectrum, not compared to what some people could do, as she knew far too well. Castigating herself for not having learned more or even followed up on this wouldn't help at this point.

At that, a man in her head whispered, *We're looking for you.*

She shifted. *Who are you?* She worked to keep her features neutral.

There was a smile in the acknowledging response. *There you are. You can hear me now, right?*

She hesitated, then asked, *Reid?*

*Yes. It's me.*

Burying her head in her arms, her shoulders shaking with sobs, she whispered in her mind, *Dear God, thank you.*

*Thank you for doing whatever you did last time. You slammed into my brain with a sledgehammer*, he shared. *Although I'm a receiver, and you are a transmitter, it only ever really seemed to work when it was the two of us.*

*Exactly, so you're the only person I knew to try to contact.*

*You have reached me, and we are trying to find you, but I really don't know where you are.*

*Neither do I*, she whispered in her mind. *I've been kept drugged, only awake this last time, as they allowed my mother to come see me.*

*Is she okay?*

*I'm not saying she's okay, but she's alive*, she clarified. *I'm under video surveillance, so I'm hiding my face while I talk to you—until I figure out how to talk in my head and not through my mouth.*

*Good. Keep it schooled the entire time that we communicate. Otherwise—*

*I know*, she cut him off. *That's what they're after. If they see any sort of proof that I can do this, things will escalate quickly.*

*How did you get yourself into this mess?*

*My mother*, she whispered. *I'm not discussing it right now. I need to get out of here, and I need to get out of here fast. Can you contact the authorities? Like MI6?*

*They're already aware of what's happened, and a plan is being formulated, but we can't do a rescue if we can't find you.*

She fell silent at that. *I have no memories of what happened*, she shared. *I wondered if they kept me drugged so I couldn't remember and tell people.*

*That would make sense.*

*Listen. If I disappear from this conversation suddenly, it's because he was just asking me whether I was talking to somebody earlier,* she murmured.

*Interesting,* he replied, *I gather you didn't know you were being watched.*

*I guessed that I might be and half assumed that to be true. Yet I didn't realize how much my expressions could get me in trouble.*

*You do need to be careful,* he warned. *We're looking for a vehicle that was stolen and may or may not have had something to do with where you were taken.*

She frowned at that. *I would feel better if you knew more.*

*We would feel better if we knew more,* he confirmed. *You don't remember a car, do you? You don't remember anything?*

*A car, yes,* she said. *I was led into a building under gunpoint, with my mother. We were kept in a small corner in a warehouse, with other people moving around, but I think … I think maybe four people were there the whole time. We were drugged part of the time—not so that we were unconscious, just so we weren't capable of doing much. It was like being in a zombie zone. I could see things going on around us, but I just couldn't seem to care.*

*Which kept you compliant and easy to manipulate.*

*Yeah, it did. And then when we got here, it seemed like they were afraid I could do things and kept me drugged again. Particularly after my mother was in here, when it seemed as if I was talking to somebody. And I was—talking to somebody, I mean. I don't know who, so now I'm afraid it was one of them.*

*It's possible, but it could also be your mind playing tricks.*

She winced. *I was hoping somebody else out there was pow-*

*erful enough to reach me.*

*That could be true as well. We certainly have a large network of people who could do what we do.*

*Really?* she asked, her body shifting, then she immediately stilled again. *Damn, talking to you like this is dangerous.*

*I can stop anytime. Do you want me to leave?*

*No! It's been so damn lonely, not to mention scary. I don't want you to go.*

*Yet I can't stay here all the time, based on energy expenditure alone. Seriously we are in Kazakhstan hunting for you.*

*Kazakhstan,* she whispered, her mind going blank at that. *Kazakhstan.*

*Do you have any connection here? Do you know anybody? Any company here? Anything?*

*Wait. One of the companies that worked with my mother was headquartered in Kazakhstan.*

*Do you know the name of it?* he asked, his tone sharp.

*I'm trying to remember, but it's not really coming up.*

*Okay, so you and she worked for the Russian government. And some suppliers may be based out of Kazakhstan. What kind of supplies would you need for your lab?*

*Medical equipment,* Veni murmured. *Something along the line of medical equipment.*

*Can you remember any contact name?*

She thought hard for a moment. *Yeah, I think it was Kenneth, but I'm not sure.*

*Okay, we'll take a look. If we get any lead, we need to double-check it first.*

*Why the devil would you go to Kazakhstan? I don't even know if I'm there.*

A chuckle came. *Yeah, well, somebody else told us to come here.*

*I hope they know what they're talking about,* she muttered, *because I don't have a clue.*

*And that's okay,* he assured her. *Just know that we're on it, and you need to stay healthy. You need to stay alive, and we'll get to you as soon as we can. If you come up with anything that reminds you of where you could be, where you might be, where you could have gone, just let me know. I presume they're planning on taking you back to Moscow?*

*That's what I've assumed. One guard told me that my mom wasn't doing so well, so she can't travel yet. That's why we're sitting in limbo at the moment, so I hope you can get to us here because it'll be that much harder to get out of Russia.*

*Yet, in some ways, it might be easier.*

She shifted. *Do you think so?*

*Maybe not, since you'll be under so much security.*

*So, why else would they wait?*

*I don't know, unless they're prepping a place to take you. It would be distressing if we lost you at this point.*

*Don't say that,* she snapped. *I can't go back there. Don't you understand?*

*I do understand,* he replied calmly, *and, when this is over, I'm looking forward to saying hi again.*

She felt a smile in his tone. *How is it we ever lost touch?* she muttered.

*For one thing, you didn't want anything to do with this psychic stuff,* he pointed out, with a note of humor. *Meanwhile, I was fascinated and wanted as much of it as I could get.*

*It scared me,* she admitted. *I didn't like the idea of people in my head.*

*Yeah, and how about now?*

*Right, point taken,* she muttered. *Now it's just so great to know that you're there and that you can hear me. It gives me immeasurable comfort.*

*Good*, he replied. *Hold that thought. We're coming. I have to go now.*

And, with that, he quickly disappeared from her mind, leaving her curled up, dry-eyed, and, for the first time since this kidnapping, with hope in her heart that maybe, just maybe, there would be a way out of this nightmare for good.

REID TURNED TO look at Anders, as they pulled into the junkyard. "I just made contact," he shared, amazement in his tone.

Anders hit the brakes hard, then turned and looked at him. "With Veni?"

"Yeah, with Veni. She's terrified and exhausted, but she is okay, and her mother is alive as well. They don't have a clue where they are. They've been separated, and she's been kept drugged most of the time. She's afraid that it's because they have a good idea of what she can do, although she says she can't do very much. She always had that belief before, which impeded her ability to thrive with this type of work."

"Okay, so can we get back to the facts?" Anders asked. "Where is she, and how will we find her?"

"She doesn't know, but she did say that, if we're in Kazakhstan, a company is headquartered here, which is likely a supplier for the Russian government, where she and her mother worked."

At that, Anders immediately sat up straighter, then pulled out his phone. "I'll get Levi on that."

"While you do that," Reid said, "I'll make contact with Terk. Let's ensure we're out of sight for the moment."

Anders pulled the vehicle forward and around the corner in a grove of trees, with the junkyard just ahead, but they were somewhat hidden here, while the two of them quickly updated their respective teams on their phones.

As he explained what happened to Terk, Reid added, "She says somebody else is talking to her. Was that you?"

"No, it wasn't," Terk replied, a puzzled note in his tone. "I could definitely feel buzzing on the ethers, but so much of this activity has been going on lately, I couldn't tell where it was coming from."

"If it wasn't you, and it wasn't me, we have another player in the game, and that is concerning."

"So she thought it might be a trap?"

"Yes, because what they've been trying to get from her is the details of what she can do, what she can't do, and who she can do it with. If they have any idea that I can connect with her and that, between us, we can talk and pass information, I'll be hunted as well."

"All the more reason for you to stay low and out of trouble then," Terk noted. "The last thing we need is you caught up in this."

"I already am in many ways, and I won't get out of it, not until we get her safely out of there."

At that, a smile filled his tone, as Terk calmly replied, "Understood."

Reid wasn't sure what that meant, but it didn't matter right now. "Anders is contacting Levi to see if anybody can roust up a medical supplier for the Russian government based out of Kazakhstan. Veni thought *Kenneth* was possibly part of the contact person's name. Unfortunately it's quite likely there could be more than one Russian medical supplier here."

"Quite likely, yes," Terk agreed. "If you think about it, it just makes sense. Unless they have somebody else within Russia who can do the same job, then why Kazakhstan versus anybody out of Russia?" he asked. "But we're on it. I'll connect with Levi, and we'll get back to you."

When Reid ended the call, he turned to see Anders waiting for him.

"You ready?" Anders asked.

"Yeah, I am. I just updated Terk," he shared. "What I didn't get a chance to tell you was Veni responded to another voice in her head. She didn't get any ID on it, and she's afraid that it was a trap, so she spoke a little bit telepathically to this guy but is even now questioning whether it was her imagination."

Anders raised an eyebrow at that. "And that matters why?"

"Because, if it's a trap, then anybody in communication with her is now potentially in danger."

"Meaning that, if they find out she can do what she's saying she can do, but maybe only with you, then you become their next intended target."

"Something like that, yeah. So, obviously we need to get her before her kidnappers figure out who's connecting with her, if anybody is, and who might be in the know about it."

"If it is a trap, it would suggest that they have somebody on their staff who also has these skills."

"And, if you think about it, that's not all that hard to believe," Reid noted. "I am one of many who I imagine are on Terk's team. Plus plenty of others must be out there somewhere."

"Too many, as far as I can tell," Anders teased, with a headshake. "I didn't think Terk would ever manage to have a team outside of the team he came with. Yet, from the sounds of things, he keeps finding other people."

"That's the thing though, because there really isn't all that many of us, so we do find group-settings appealing. It's become a support system, but, more than that, it's also a security system," he admitted. "None of us want to become victims of all these people who seem to think we're just for their entertainment or for greed or power or whatever. Or, in this case, for their pet projects or to become pawns in their dominance game."

"That is even more disconcerting," Anders muttered.

"Exactly, because we don't know how many psychics and the like that the Russians may have on staff or whether they can track Veni's communications."

"Track her or track you?" Anders asked, with a pointed look. "Maybe keep the communication with her to a minimum, since we have no idea how far this shit goes."

Reid winced at that. "I hear you, but it's a little hard to do that, especially when I know she's terrified and alone."

"I get that too," Anders replied, "but you won't be of any help to her if you don't survive yourself." Anders opened the driver's side door and stated, "Let's go check out this stolen car."

As they walked toward the junkyard, leaving their vehicle a block behind in the trees, Reid added, "I presume things here run like anywhere else, where enough money gets us answers."

"Yeah, but it can also bring a lot of interest that we don't want," Anders shared. "We've already brought in some interest with our unorthodox arrival," he noted, looking at him.

"Yeah, sorry about that."

He shrugged. "I'm not really. It was definitely new to me, but it served its purpose in that we're finding a stolen vehicle that apparently nobody is willing to tell the old man about."

"Or he knows and doesn't like it because he's broke and now without a car, which he just paid to have tuned up."

"Yep, that's another viable option," Anders agreed, with a nod.

"And, if somebody didn't like the angry old man, maybe they wanted to teach him a lesson, and maybe that is their way of doing it."

"*Great.* You know it really pisses me off when people treat our seniors like that."

"Maybe, but I would hold your sympathy for the moment. My team is doing a rundown on that old man, and apparently he's got a long criminal record."

"Ah, well, that's just wonderful," he muttered, with a groan. "You never can tell with anybody, can you?"

"No, but, for me, it depends on what he did. If it was stealing bread to feed children, I won't hold it against him. That's a whole different story."

They walked into the junkyard only to find nobody was there to greet them. Frowning, they wandered around, looking for the vehicle.

"Shouldn't somebody be here?"

"Maybe, yet anybody who deliberately set us on the path as to where this stolen vehicle was may not expect us to show up here."

"Yet you would think they would be expecting somebody."

They wandered around the place, found the vehicle in question, and double-checked the license plate.

"This is it. What do you expect to find?" Anders asked.

Reid smiled. "With any luck, some sign that Veni was in here."

"Go for it," Anders said. "I'll stand lookout." And, with that, Anders moved a few feet away, while Reid stepped closer and started to search the vehicle.

He wasn't sure what he would find or even what he could find at this point. The vehicle had clearly held a lot of people over time and distance, but, if there were anything to find, he wanted to ensure he did. It didn't take long before he pulled out a stack of napkins from between the seats.

The trouble was, napkins didn't prove anything. Sure, they were covered in DNA, but it would take time to sort out who had been there and who hadn't. When he pulled out a business card, it was for a company that sold medical supplies. He sat back, looked at it, then, taking the napkins with him, did another quick search, finding another napkin jammed up on the other side. He opened it to see a single word.

Help.

*Bingo.*

# CHAPTER 7

NOW THAT VENI had connected with Reid, all she could do was wait in anticipation, hoping somebody would get her and her mother out of this mess. Veni had no way to let her mother know that things were looking up. Veni was also even more confused about the unidentified voice she had heard earlier. Whether it was helpful or a trick, she didn't know, but she was wary.

She would talk to Reid, but this other man? No way. It crossed her mind briefly that maybe Reid himself had been a trick of her mind or even a setup by the government. It wasn't beyond them to have dragged through her history and found Reid in there. When Reid spoke to her and mentioned several things about her not wanting to pursue this field, that had convinced her more than anything that he was legit because he'd been gung-ho about this, yet not sure where to go and how to go about doing it, yet open to the idea, whereas she had been the polar opposite.

She didn't want anything to do with it, not seeing any real purpose, and she had been honest when she had admitted that it scared her. The thought of a boogeyman in the night coming at her from a direction she couldn't even see wasn't something she wanted to consider. Whereas Reid had been all over the idea that, at least this way, they would see it coming. She didn't see his point of view back then.

Since they hadn't had a whole lot of connection other than that, they had drifted apart, or maybe that was more about her, as she had just slammed the door on him. She'd been good at that back then. All about denial, all about her way or the highway, though that hadn't gone that well for her either. Only when she hooked up with her mom to help her out with her research did Veni realize the potential for a larger purpose with her gift. It had been the first time she'd had any inkling of the import of what she could do and what it could be applied to.

When she'd realized that she could transmit messages to cells, it had quickly all become something beyond her comprehension. Even her mother had stared at her for a long time, wanting to test her, to open up her brain, and to figure out what made her tick. It had taken a lot to convince even her own mother that this was something that had to be done gently and carefully. Otherwise it would likely harm Veni.

She knew her mom would never hurt her on purpose, but Veni hadn't been the most cooperative in terms of assisting her mom either. Veni felt bad about that now too. All she seemed to be doing was feeling guilty, and that wasn't productive. She wanted to bang her head against the wall, like some SOS signal, hoping to get somebody in here to free her and her mom. Yet all she could do was sit in silence and wait.

When the door opened a little while later, she stared with dull eyes at the guard, the one missing a tooth.

Her jailer frowned at her. "You don't look too good."

She didn't say anything, just turned her gaze to the wall. Better that they thought she was getting sick or depressed at the very least, and she didn't even have to put on an act for that. The lack of daylight, the lack of any decent food for days now, all took its toll. She had always been a very active person, and this captivity wasn't her usual state, yet they wouldn't care. They wouldn't care about anything, unless it affected her ability to do what they wanted her to do.

"Somebody is here to see you," he announced.

She shifted her gaze back to the door and his face. "My mother?"

"No, not your mother. Somebody else."

And with that, her jailer—the one playing games with her, talking about *cooperation*, yeah, right—stepped into her room. She had absolutely no interest in seeing him again. She needed to come up with a name for them, just to separate them out. The normal guard, the one who fed her, who had led her mother in, she would call Toothless because he was missing a big front tooth. But this guy? Well, she didn't think he was the boss, but he definitely had that persona, so *the Boss* he was. She waited for him to say something.

"Your mother is willing to cooperate," he began, "to come back to the job that she had and to continue working in her field. We want you to come back with her."

She stared at him. "Why would she do that?"

"That's easy," he replied, "because we assured her that we would let you live."

She winced. "Yeah, that's pretty-well guaranteed to get any mother's cooperation, isn't it?"

He laughed. "We're not above using whatever force we need to make this happen. We really don't want you to suffer. You don't look like you're doing all that well."

"No fresh air, no daylight, no decent food?" She shrugged. "What did you expect?"

He frowned at her. "The food's not that bad."

"I wouldn't know because I haven't gotten very much of it," she noted, looking at him in surprise. "A couple sandwiches over a few days, and that's it." She watched anger build on his face and noted that he hadn't known. "Maybe your jailer is pocketing the money that you're giving him, keeping it for himself. I mean, after all, I'm just a prisoner, right? Why should I get any special treatment, like decent food to keep me alive and my brain functioning?" she asked.

He disappeared quickly after that, and she heard yelling but couldn't hear what was said, although she had a pretty good idea what had set it off.

About an hour later, her door opened again. Toothless came in, glaring at her. "Complaining about the food, are you?" he snarled. "Don't worry. I'll remember that."

"I didn't complain about anything. He asked me what I had to eat, and I told him the plain and simple truth."

He looked at her, uncertain, but slammed the tray down on the table and quickly disappeared.

She got up slowly and walked over, surprised to see more food than normal and of slightly better quality. She would take it because, right now, she needed everything she could to replenish her energy to get out of here.

A hint of dark suspicion arose in the back of her mind, which she didn't dare put any thought into. Still, when she was calmer, when she was ready, when she had a chance to consider who was behind all this, Veni would have to take a closer look at that suspicion. If she ended up wrong, that was perfect, but if she were right? ... Well, it would break her heart.

"WHAT IS IT we're thinking is happening here?" Terk asked Reid on the phone.

His cell was on Speaker, and Reid and Anders sat in their rental vehicle. "Somebody wrote *help* on a napkin, so whether that was just a joke from somebody else, I don't know," Reid related. "We dropped everything off at the local lab, as per your instructions." He shook his head and added, "Now we're just sitting here, waiting, trying to formulate a plan for where to go from here. Did you get any research back on the company?"

"Yes, I have it for you. They've been running supplies for the Russian government for quite a few years now," he said.

Reid replied, "So anybody who's worked there probably has a good relationship with them."

Terk agreed. "That makes sense. In order to keep a business like this, you want to keep your suppliers happy. Now, whether that relationship was with the mother or the government itself, I don't know. We're still checking on that."

Reid asked, "Veni's father also worked for the government, didn't he?"

"Yes, he did, although he's in a very different location, and apparently they're separated."

"Interesting," he murmured.

"Why?" Terk asked.

"Just ... I wondered if he could be involved in some way."

"It's possible. I mean, the two of them are separated. I don't know anything about those circumstances because we don't have any of the related personal details."

"But we do have this company address, so that's where

we will go next," Anders stated, as he fired up the car, "because we're not getting very far just parked here, like sitting ducks."

"The DNA will come back fairly quickly. If it is Veni and her mom, then we're right on track," Terk noted.

"Honestly I believe we're on track just because of Langdon's involvement," Reid admitted. "Does he want to fire up that instinct of his again and give us some directions as to where to find her? If she's here, the best thing would be that we locate her and fast."

"Right," Terk admitted. "I'm also trying to figure out who else may have telecommunicated with her."

"Yeah, that's another concern," Reid agreed, "but not the most prevalent one at the moment. We need to find her and get her out of there, while we still can."

"Have you talked to her since?"

"No, but I was wondering about it," he shared, casting a glance at Anders. "Anders is afraid that, if I do, whoever this other voice belongs to will track us backward."

"*Hmm.*" Terk pondered that. "I hate to say it, but it's quite possible, and Anders is looking out for you—and all of us really. So, he may not be wrong."

"No, he might not be wrong, but that doesn't mean I have any other option."

"Try it again. Do you know how to find out if you have a tracker?"

"No, I sure don't," he said. "I do what I do, but I don't have any training in any of the rest of it."

"If you survive this," Terk replied, with a note of humor, "we can do something about that. Yet, for the moment, we're kind of stuck with whatever we have to work with."

"So basically, not a whole lot," he muttered.

"Try to contact her again and ask if she left the napkins in that vehicle. We should get the DNA back very quickly. Get to the offices of that company, and let's see if she could be held there. When you're there, text me, and I'll see if I can get Langdon to tap in. He's been trying. Don't get me wrong, but it's not always something we can switch on all the time."

"That's the thing I've never quite understood," Anders added. "The information, when we get it, is great, but it's not something we can count on getting."

"It never is," Terk agreed. "But, as you said, when we can get it, it's golden, and we need some of that right now." And, with that, he signed off.

Anders punched in the address they'd been given. "Okay, let's head to that medical supply company."

"Yeah, I'm ready," Reid shared.

"Will you contact her?" Anders asked.

"I've been trying for the last few minutes, but either she's asleep or she's unconscious again."

At that, Anders nodded. "If she were my prisoner and if I thought she could do something like this, I would probably keep her unconscious too. Maybe for a lot longer than usual."

# CHAPTER 8

WHEN VENI WOKE up, she was groggy, her tongue thick. When she muttered, "What the hell," her tone was raspy. She realized right away that the better food she'd been given had been laced with drugs. That's why she'd been given so much and such a variety in order to disguise the taste. This confirmed that they were afraid she was communicating with someone, or else it was some sort of a lesson.

She didn't know which.

She'd been drugged before, and that had made it much harder to communicate. Now she didn't know what to think. She wished she could see her mom again, but that was also a torment because she couldn't get her out of here. Her mother didn't appear to be suffering terribly though, and that was a good thing, but she was also a highly respected microbiologist. Yet her stem cell research was a little bit out of her field. However, since she had made such incredible breakthroughs, nobody would argue against her value of doing any work.

They also wanted her to continue with her stem cell work, hence this mess presumably. Veni wasn't even sure what to do about that. As the day wore on, she wished she had some water. That was one thing they always kept from her, and she could really use it, especially with her tongue tasting the way it did. The door opened suddenly, and her jailer, Toothless, walked in, glaring at her still.

"What? So you didn't like the questions he asked, so you drugged me again?" she asked bitterly. "Good thing they don't want me to do anything, since the drugs are killing any chance of that."

Startled, he looked at her for a long moment and didn't say anything but slammed the tray down and quickly disappeared. She didn't know if she'd scared him enough that he would lay off the drugs or if he was just following orders, more than happy to send the drugs into her bloodstream and to shut her up.

She'd tried not being difficult, and she'd tried not getting too mouthy, but she was getting fed up and really just wanted Reid to get her the hell out of here. That thought wasn't helping her either. As she reached for the bottle of water, she studied it and found the seal had been broken. Frowning, she put it back down again and stared at it. She needed water. If they had just reused a bottle—which would make sense if they didn't have supplies—and didn't add any drugs, that was one thing. The other thing was, what were her options when she needed liquids in her body. Still, she put the water bottle off to the side and didn't touch it, eyeing the rest of the food on the plate, already hesitant to try anything.

When Toothless returned a little later, staring at her untouched food and water, he asked in an aggrieved tone, "What's the matter with the food this time?"

"You probably drugged it again," she snapped, with a wave of her hand. "I can't trust you."

He stared at her, and she watched his face work with fury but didn't know which of several options were the cause. Was it because of the drugs in the food or because he was angry at her for having doubted him? Or that the drugs had to be given to her, and, if she wouldn't cooperate, she would get injected with them. She wouldn't make anything easy on them anymore. She closed her eyes, and he picked up the tray and disappeared.

When Toothless returned with the boss man, she nodded. "So, it was drugged, and now I have absolutely no say in it?" she asked in a mocking tone. "Do whatever," she muttered. "And if it renders me unconscious permanently, that's all the better."

At that, the boss froze, turned to her jailer, and said something in a language she didn't quite understand. And right in front of her, an argument ensued, but she didn't need to speak the language in order to understand that it was over her being drugged.

The boss now faced her. "If you're good, I won't give you more drugs."

She stared at him in surprise. "Have I not been good?" she asked, waving an arm around her prison cell. "What is it you expect me to do? I'm already a prisoner here. I can't even go to the bathroom without asking you guys for permission. The food is all over the map. I either get no food at all, or the food that I get is drugged. I always know when it's drugged because that's the only time you give me an actual meal. Water is something I don't even get, and I'm so parched from your drugs now that it's affecting my system," she muttered. "I don't know what you expect from me, but I'm well past the point of dealing with any of it."

Worried, the boss walked over and checked her temperature, picking up her wrist, as if to check her pulse. She deliberately slowed her system, trying to throw him off. He turned and barked something at Toothless, who immediately disappeared. When he came back, he carried two sealed bottles of water in his hands. He passed them over to her, and she immediately cracked one open and gulped down some water. When she finally lowered the bottle, she whispered, "Thank you."

"We're not trying to hurt you, you know," the boss muttered in English.

She spoke Russian and several dialects, having spent many years in the country, yet the boss had returned to English. She found that interesting, since it meant that English was probably his first language. "You could have fooled me," she replied. "The food, the water, the drugs, plus no daylight, no place to wash, and nothing at all to improve my spirits, yet you want me to perform like a pony."

He winced at that. "Hey, it's not me," he declared, "but, once you piss off the government, they tend to get real hands-on in a hurry."

"Yeah, *sorry* about that," she muttered. "I never wanted to spend my life as a prisoner."

He cracked a smile. "If you changed that attitude, you wouldn't be a prisoner."

She snorted. "No? And what would I be?"

"You would be an employee." And that joke had him laughing uproariously. Then he turned and left, but he barked out more orders as he walked away. Toothless glared at her, so she assumed that he was once again in trouble or at least charged with doing more that the boss wanted Toothless to do. But she had water without drugs added, and that was worth something.

When Toothless returned later with a hot, thick soup and slabs of bread, he glared at her and said, in Russian, "It's not drugged." Then he left.

She wasn't sure whether she could believe him or not, but the thick bread would be hard to drug, right? So she ate that first, while she studied the soup. It looked to be fresh and was very tempting. When she didn't eat it, a doctor came in, at least she assumed he was a doctor, with his white coat. He came with his own spoon and ate several bites of the soup himself, as if to demonstrate it wasn't drugged. Then he left as well. Knowing that she was being watched, she cautiously took a couple bites and then polished off the bowl and the rest of the bread. Cracking open the second bottle of water, she had some of that as well.

She needed to go to the bathroom again, and, so far, she had a bucket, or she asked, if she wanted to deal with the guards. But now, knowing that she was being watched all the time, she sure didn't want to use the bucket. Not to mention the smell, since they didn't clean it out or even give a crap. She'd used it to throw up a time or two, and that was still sitting here as well.

About an hour later Toothless came and led her to the bathroom, where she relieved herself and quickly washed her hands and her face. There was no mirror, which was probably so she couldn't break the glass and use it as a weapon. When he opened the door on her, a bit surprised, she was still scrubbing her face. He waited for her to finish, then led her back to her cell, where he closed the door once again. There, she sank into despair.

Although she was feeling better and had a full stomach, just knowing she was back in this windowless room again, after being out even for those few minutes, was heartbreaking. She sent out a desperate plea to Reid. *Please be coming.*

She got an instant response.

*Yes, we're coming.*

With a smile on her face, she fell asleep.

REID PROBABLY SHOULDN'T have told her that, but she needed to know that they were on it. He didn't tell anybody that he had kept up communication with her, as more of a point of reassurance for her than anything. He was also trying to figure out who else was telecommunicating with Veni too.

That was a concern, and it was also a concern for another reason, and he wasn't sure anybody else had picked up on it. He quickly sent Terk a text, asking what were chances the voice in her head was another prisoner. Terk sent a response that made Reid's blood run cold.

"I'm pretty sure it is."

Of course that meant that they not only had to rescue Veni and her mom but somebody else. Reid told Terk that as well, and his response came back immediately.

"I'm on it."

Reid had to smile at that. An awful lot could be said about somebody who would rescue someone else who was gifted, yet being held prisoner because of what they could do—especially knowing it wasn't a job or something he got paid for. Yet Terk did it because it was the right thing to do.

Reid sat back in the car, as they pulled into the parking lot of the medical supply house, and stared. "Where is everybody?"

"It is the weekend," Anders replied.

"Oh." Reid shook his head. "Wow, I've really lost track of time."

"That's all right. I'm on it."

"I'm glad you are. I don't have the level of experience in this sort of thing that you do."

"Which is why we make a decent team," Anders stated, with a smile, "because I don't have any experience in the crap you're dealing with."

Reid burst out laughing. "Very true."

"Now text Terk and see if he's got anything to offer."

"I've been talking to him this last bit." He smirked and added, "Telepathically. Still, we do need to see if Langdon's got any directions for us."

"Levi just sent me the blueprints for the place as well because I would really like to know if this is empty for the weekend. There is also another aspect. What are the chances that Veni's being held here? If she and her mother are here, maybe they're someplace where nobody would even run across them because it's not a regular part of everybody's workspace. I'm thinking like an old factory, a warehouse, some storage barns, and things like that."

"She's warm enough, but she has a blanket," Reid shared.

"You contacted her? Did she tell you that?"

He hesitated and then shook his head. "No, I'll just say it's an impression."

Anders shot him a look. "When you get confirmation of that …"

"Right." Reid grinned. "You're really all about facts, aren't you?"

"I am, and you're really all about impressions and feel-ings."

"It's a lot of the work I do," he admitted, "although it's not even *work*-work."

"What were you doing before?"

"I took care of artillery for years, but I left the military about two years ago, after being pretty upset with what was going on. I was an artillery master, but you know there's only so much of that you can do before you wonder why you're even doing it."

"Been there, done that," Anders stated. "It's one of the reasons I do this now because I couldn't before."

Reid recognized the resolve in his tone. "You mean, making decisions and helping people when the government won't? Because, in this case, the government is definitely involved."

"Which reminds me, we haven't had any feedback from Jonas in a while."

"Good point," Reid noted. "Let me send Terk a message about that."

When his phone buzzed not too much later, Terk shared how Jonas had supplied some of the information about this company. He also stated that the person they communicated with in terms of getting the women out in the first place had gone missing two days after connecting with the women, and another body was just found in a back alley.

"*Great*, so they're making sure that nobody is available for us to question."

"Exactly, and, of course, that's not a surprise, but it does raise the stakes a bit."

"Yeah, it also means that anybody involved in hiding these women may just get wiped out. Or already has been."

"Exactly, and yet the old man's car was potentially used, and he is still alive—or was alive that day—which may explain the visitor he had there that morning."

"Yeah, I would like to have a talk with him again," Reid

muttered. "That was definitely a curiosity. Plus I can confirm if he's still alive."

"Maybe he is, since he certainly put out the alert to his bosses that people were asking for the women, and the people had made it as far as Kazakhstan, which must also be a concern for the Russians," Terk murmured. "Yet I'm thinking he's dead. If you get more people on your tail, we need to know about it because I sure don't like surprises."

"I suggest we just take that as a blanket statement and assume we have more people on our tail than we expected," Reid replied, half joking.

As they walked up to the front of the building, Anders flicked through images on his phone.

"Blueprints?" Reid asked.

"Yeah, blueprints. Of course the building's closed, and there is security presumably, but, on the surface, I'm not seeing any cars in the parking lot or nearby."

"It's probably no more than what we would consider regular security on a weekend," Reid pointed out, "so maybe no security at all."

He snorted at that. "Also, business hasn't been very good lately, so maybe the security part is something that went by the wayside."

"Maybe. I don't know. … I suggest we scale the gate and go around the other side," he muttered.

"Or," Anders offered, "just pop the lock on this gate and go in and out the front."

"Yet that will let somebody know because cameras should be around here."

With that, they quickly skirted the perimeter, looking for a place to get in. Along the back fence, where the garbage came and went, was a gate. It was only held closed by a chain.

"I've never quite understood why people are so lax about places like this." Reid shook his head.

"It's not even that they're lax," Anders reminded him, "but people who cart off the garbage must really get pissed with locks and keypads. I bet they really don't give a crap and don't see any point of it being secure. It's not as if this is some super-high-security espionage farm, so, from their point of view, closing up a gate like this is minor."

And, indeed, it was minor, just a simple chain, which they unwound instantly, and were inside. They quickly looped the chain back around the gate again, so, from a quick glance, nobody would know that they had entered. With that, they dashed to the loading docks and studied the layout.

"According to the blueprints, this loading dock will let us in on the ground floor. It goes down one more floor for storage and up two floors to manufacturing and offices."

"Good enough," Reid said. "I'll go down. You go up."

At that, Anders looked over at him, his lips twitching. "How about we reverse that? I'll go down, and you go up."

"In that case, why don't we just stay together," Reid replied, with a laugh.

Within seconds, they were inside the building, and they both had weapons out at the ready. As soon as they cleared the main floor, they shared a look. "The fastest thing would be to clear upstairs, but being offices, they're not holding anybody there, not through a workweek at least," Reid shared. "My bet would be downstairs."

"Mine too."

And with that settled, they quickly took the stairs down below the loading dock into the storage area. As soon as they got down there, Reid felt energy wafting in. He reached out and grabbed Anders by the arm. "Something's going on here."

Anders waited, looking at him. "When you say that, what do you mean?"

He shook his head. "I know you're looking for absolutes in this, and, as much as I would like to give you some, I just don't have them."

"Then tell me what this means to you, at least."

He contemplated the area for a moment and then nodded. "It means that somebody has been using energy here."

"Okay, is that good or bad?" Anders asked cautiously.

"I want to say good because I think it's probably Veni, but there's an awful lot of it."

"Meaning?"

"I'm not sure," Reid admitted in exasperation. "Maybe check in with Terk."

"Oh no, no, no, no," Anders said. "*You* check in with Terk. I only talk to Terk when he's got something to say to me."

He snorted. "You don't think he would have something to say right now?"

"If he did, he would already be on the phone."

That was an indisputable truth, so moving cautiously forward, the two of them came up to a junction that led down a dark hallway with multiple doors on either side. Reid pointed left.

Anders whispered in a low tone, "Is that your buddy telling you left again?"

"Nope, just me following my instincts."

Anders nodded. "In that case, I don't have a problem following it. Instincts have kept me alive more than a few times."

They moved slowly, cautiously, down to the other doors. As they came to the first one, Reid put an ear against it and couldn't hear anything going on. They kept on going to the second one, same thing. Third one, same thing. When they got to the fourth one, there he heard voices, and it sounded like a TV was on. "Maybe the jailers," he whispered.

He looked over at Anders who motioned to carry on down to the next door to see if they could find the hostages. Security should be here, and this could just as easily be the security room. Cameras could be in there, or nothing but somebody who needed a place for the weekend. They kept on walking past door after door after door, until finally they came up to the last one, where Reid tilted his head and pointed.

Anders just shrugged, as if not seeing what he was pointing out, but it was energy and a lot of it. He pointed toward the room and nodded. At that, he tried the handle, but it was locked. Quickly taking a tool from his pocket, he had the lock undone within seconds, then pushed open the door. They both stepped inside and closed it behind them, and there in front of them was a woman curled up on a bed, sound asleep.

He raced over to her side and checked, then looked back at Anders and whispered, "It's not Veni."

Shocked, he stared at him and asked, "What?"

He nodded. "This isn't Veni." Matter of fact, she was older. He looked at her closely and then added, "I think it's probably her mother." He checked for a pulse, but she was sleeping soundly, completely undisturbed by their actions. "By the looks of it, I think she's been drugged."

"That'll complicate matters," Anders shared. "I was really hoping they'd both be ambulatory."

"You might be hoping, but, in this case, you'll be disappointed." He looked at the door. "We need to find Veni."

With that, they stepped back out into the hallway and headed across the hall to the closest door. Reid looked at the energy and nodded. When Anders popped the lock, they stepped inside, their weapons at the ready, and found another woman curled up in a ball on an inflatable mattress, sleeping. He raced over to her side.

He placed two fingers at her neck, turning her face gently so he could look at her, then he glanced back at Anders and smiled. "It's Veni."

She murmured something.

He reached out a hand and gave her a gentle shake. When she didn't respond, he gave her a harder shake. She woke up, glaring at him. Then her eyes widened, and she scrambled out of his reach, pulling the blanket up tight.

His heart broke for what she had gone through, but he reached out a hand again and whispered, "Veni, it's me. It's Reid."

# CHAPTER 9

VENI STARED AT Reid in disbelief, the vestiges of sleep falling away from her brain. Bolting to her feet, she threw herself into his arms, tears pouring down her cheeks. When she saw another man behind him, she stiffened.

Reid held her tightly against himself and whispered, "It's okay. He's with me. This is Anders."

She shuddered and nodded, then looking over at Anders, she mouthed, *Thank you.*

He just nodded in return.

Reid studied her and asked, "Have you been drugged? Are you okay? Ambulatory? Are you hurt?"

"I'm fine," she whispered, "but I don't know for how long."

"We get that," he replied. "We haven't found your guards, although we think we know what room they're in, and we did find your mother."

Her eyes lit with hope. "Really?"

"Come on. We have to get you out of here."

Moving silently, they headed back to the room where her mother was, with the door still unlocked. Anders went in and scooped up the older woman and carried her out so that Veni could see.

Tears in her eyes, Veni gently stroked her mother's face. "Is she okay?" she whispered.

"I hope so," Reid said, "but we must get you both out of here, and we need to do it now."

She nodded, and with Veni holding Reid's hand, they slipped past the guardroom, where they heard the TV still going.

Farther down the hallway, just as they headed toward the main area where the exit and the loading dock stairs were, a shout came from behind them. Reid looked back at Anders, with a grim expression.

Anders nodded. "Now it's a free-for-all time, and we have to move it. We've lost that element of surprise." With Anders still carrying Veni's mom, he picked up the pace in a fast run, racing for the stairs. Holding hands, Reid and Veni raced up behind them. She knew that, if they got caught, there was no hope for any of them. She quickly dismissed that thought and wouldn't even consider that right now, not when their rescue was so close at hand.

She didn't even know how Reid had found her, but the fact that he was here meant a lot to her. As they ran outside, nobody was there to greet them. Stumbling, Veni followed Reid around the back of the building, and she felt herself tiring. The moment she felt that lag, energy poured into her system. In surprise, she watched her feet just pick up on their own accord, racing faster and faster. They came to a fence and a locked gate, but they quickly had it open and were out on the other side right where their vehicle was parked. She collapsed in the middle of the back seat with Reid to her right and her mom to her left, as Anders popped into the driver's seat. They ripped out of that parking lot, just ahead of a barrage of bullets flying in their direction. Several pinged off the vehicle, but they were too far away to do any damage. Reid, in the back seat with her, turned and opened his arms.

She crawled into them and burst into tears.

"It's okay, we made it out," Reid murmured.

"We're out, but they'll be after us like crazy now."

"Yeah, but they were before too," Anders noted comfortably. "I'm an old hand at this, so I won't say we're out of the woods because we definitely aren't, but you're in a hell of a lot better position now than you were merely minutes ago."

She smiled at Anders gratefully and, from the circle of Reid's arms, whispered, "Thank you, thank you, thank you."

Anders eyed her in the rearview mirror and gave her a chin lift. Reid just nodded and squeezed her tight.

She smiled and looked back up at him, then grabbed him by the cheeks and gave him a big kiss. "You were right. I'll admit it," she shared. "I should have developed these skills a long time ago."

"You should have," he agreed, with a gentle smile, holding her close. "It would have been a hell of a lot easier to find you."

She sighed. "Whoever would have thought that this would be something I would get into?"

"At least now you're out of it."

"Maybe," she murmured. "However, I'll never sleep again, not without those nightmares cracking through my brain, telling me that I'm in danger."

"PTSD is a real thing," he acknowledged. "And, until you can get past it, honor the nightmares," he suggested. "Right now we're definitely not out of danger, and we need to ditch this vehicle, find another, and keep on moving." At that, he looked over at Anders, one eyebrow raised.

With a nod, Anders stated, "We need air support. While you get on that, I'll find a shopping mall and maybe hot-wire another vehicle we can transfer to. Then we're out of here."

Veni listened to the men on their phones, as she crawled closer to her mother to wrap her up in a hug. "It's okay, Mom," she whispered. "We're out. You're safe."

But her mom remained in a deeply drugged state.

Veni gently pulled the hair off her mother's face and held her mom close, the tears rolling down Veni's cheeks. After everything they'd gone through, here was a rescue from a corner she hadn't even begun to think was possible. Yet somehow Reid had pulled it off. She was indebted to this man, not that he would likely give a crap, but, for her, it mattered that he had stepped up and showed up, for her and her mom. It mattered a lot.

He'd done so much in this little time span to make her realize how much value all these special gifts could be, something that she hadn't even contemplated way back when. And she was so grateful that Reid had listened to what his abilities were and had chosen to develop them. Holding her mother in her arms, while the men barked orders into their phones, Veni finally allowed herself to have that little bit of hope that they would get out of this. Hope had been a whole lot harder to muster when this day first began.

JUST AS THE foursome pulled out onto a main highway, hoping to find a mall to change cars in, a vehicle careened closer behind them.

"Hold on," Anders cried out, as he took a hard left and then a series of sharp corners, as he tried to get rid of their tail. "We definitely have to dump this vehicle now," he snapped. "We're just coming up on a parking lot, but it's not as optimal as I would have wanted."

He pulled into the back of the parking lot, parked between two bigger vehicles, and dashed away. Meanwhile, Reid lifted Veni's mother in his arms, and, with Veni beside him, he looked around to find Anders, just as he drove toward them in another vehicle. They hopped in, and he drove out of the lot the same way they had come in.

"Mission one accomplished," Reid noted. "Now get us to an airport, and maybe we can get a flight out of here and fast." Reid's phone buzzed. He quickly gave Anders directions and then more directions, and, by the time, they pulled into a small private airstrip, a plane was warming up on the tarmac. With all four of them on board, the plane quickly took to the air, just as they saw other vehicles pulling into the airstrip beside them.

Reid looked down and muttered, "*Uh-oh*, bet they're a little pissed off."

"Yeah well, they can be pissed off all they want," Veni exclaimed. "They made my life and my mother's life a living hell, and I won't forgive them for that for a long time."

He smiled. "Don't really think they'll care, sweetheart."

She smiled up at him. "No," she agreed, tears in her eyes. "They won't, but we do." She looked over at her mother. "I hope she's okay. That drugged sleep for this long is so disconcerting."

"It is, particularly when we don't know what she's been given," Reid added. "Yet I would imagine they were fairly careful, with drug selection and dosages, since they didn't want to hurt either of you. The work you guys are doing is pretty impressive, and that makes you very valuable. Both of you."

"Valuable, and yet dangerous."

"Did the Russians really know what you could do?" Anders asked, from his window seat on the airplane.

She nodded. "My mom was reporting to them, and she was of the opinion that they would care in a good way."

"Ah." Anders shook his head. "So is she still that innocent?"

"I don't know. She didn't want to leave for the longest time. Not until they started pressuring me more and more into working for them, whether I wanted to or not," she shared. "That's when I persuaded her to make this happen."

"We've already contacted MI6, but this plane itself won't take us all that far," Reid told everyone, "not to mention we don't have any cleared flight plans for getting into any of the major airports."

It was obvious from the look on Veni's face that she didn't quite understand.

He explained in a grim tone, "In other words, we're not out of danger."

She nodded. "Until we're safely back in England, I can't imagine that will be anything I can count on for a while."

"No, it won't be," Reid confirmed, "but we're getting there."

She smiled. "Thank you again for the rescue."

"We've got this," he said, with a chuckle. "We will get you out of here."

"I know you will," she declared. "I never doubted that, once we connected. The fact that we could even connect is what kept me sane in there."

"I was trying to send you messages the whole time," Reid told her, "but I never heard a response."

"I was trying to send you messages," she said, "because you're the only one I knew who could connect with me, no matter the obstacles of distance or building construction, as you were the only one who was available and who has connected with me in the past."

He chuckled. "That's one of the reasons I was trying so hard because we did have that pathway from before. I'm sure Terk would have something to say about that."

"Terk?" she repeated.

Reid smiled at her. "Somebody who can do what we do but on steroids."

Her gaze widened. "Wow. ... See? If I had met people who could do what we did, and I saw a purpose for it," she clarified, "it would have completely changed everything in my world."

"So what made you change now?"

She winced. "I transmit, but I hadn't been good at receiving, as you very well know. However, on a lark one day, I was transmitting energy to some cells in the lab—just wondering if anything was in there to communicate with, you know? I wasn't really ... I wasn't planning on anything happening. This wasn't a verified scientific experiment or anything." She shook her head. "But lo and behold I found that my actions affected the way the cells reacted, and I showed my mom the results. She got super excited because, of course, then we could affect the way the cells grew and divided, depending on how much energy I could give them. Different energy had different results, and we were playing with that a bit—but then she told people." Veni winced.

"Right, not a good idea."

"Yeah, and that completely changed everything. All the government bosses raced to the lab to figure it out and to see what we could do, and I was put on the spot to do it more vigorously. At that time I wasn't even thinking about trying to keep it quiet, so yeah I showed them. Big mistake."

"Yeah, you're not kidding." Reid eyed her strangely. "Remember the first rule? We don't tell anybody, especially people without our gifts."

"Yeah, well, nobody ever claimed that I was brilliant," she muttered.

He burst out laughing. "As I remember, you were always very brilliant," he stated, "and that was another reason why we needed to keep everything quiet."

She shook her head at that. "You were the brilliant one. I was the idiot. I'm the one who decided this stuff was not for me."

"Then you started using your gifts again, but in a lab at that. That's the part I don't get. I mean, it was fun and all to put it to the test but not in a monitored situation like that. What were you thinking?"

"Because it was for my mother, I didn't even question it," she replied. "I hadn't really played with any of this stuff since you left," she muttered. "I didn't know anybody I could even talk to about it. So what was I supposed to do? I didn't … I didn't think," she muttered, almost in tears. "I'm not so naïve about it now."

"Of course not," he declared. "That kind of thing is one of those life-altering events."

"It absolutely is," she murmured. "My mother was ecstatic because it meant she could do more with her research. Yet when I told her that I wasn't sure it was something I wanted to really focus on long-term, she wasn't happy at all."

"If you wanted to do that, you would have gone into the sciences yourself because you loved it. However, as I recall, that wasn't where your interests were."

"Not at all," she replied. "My life is really about writing. I wanted to write books," she admitted, with a laugh. "Yet I never got anywhere on that either."

"Sometimes you have to live a little before you can write a lot," he suggested, with a smile. "So don't put that out to pasture yet."

"I'm not," she said. "Right now I definitely feel that I have a lot more to experience and a lot more to write about, but it'll take a while to find my new normal. This was pretty painful stuff."

"It was," he agreed, giving her a big hug again. "But hold that thought, as we're getting there."

"We're on a plane, heading somewhere other than where I was being held captive," she noted. "I'll take all of that as progress." She gently kissed him on the cheek. "Thank you."

The problem was, as he stared at her, his love for her exposed in his gaze, he didn't want gratitude.

His other problem was, this feeling he'd had for her all these years ago hadn't gone away.

Those feelings had been asleep, now reawakening, while she was near.

# CHAPTER 10

T HE FOUR OF them were on their third flight, this one taking them to England, and now they had a doctor on board to boot. Veni watched as the latest addition to their group worked on her mother. Veni sat close by, holding her mother's hand. "Will she be okay?" she asked the doctor, for at least the tenth time.

The doctor nodded and smiled at her, patiently explaining, "It's just the drugs. She's sleeping them off," he stated reassuringly.

She sat back at Reid's nudge and looked over at him.

Reid murmured, "Give her body a chance to let the drugs run their course. She's in good hands."

Veni nodded but kept casting wary glances toward the doctor.

Finally Reid grabbed her gently by the arm and tucked her closer. "Maybe you should get a nap." She glared at him, but he smiled back. "When you were drugged, you just slept it off, so no need to worry."

"Yeah?"

"Right now, that's what your mom needs to do. We'll get her fully checked out, now that we know that this is mostly due to the drugs. Once we hit England, you'll be taken to a hospital as well to get checked over even further."

"Maybe we should have stopped somewhere else," she

argued. He gave her a pointed look, and she winced. "I know. I know. I'm the one who insisted on coming straight here," she murmured. "I just wanted to get some distance from that nightmare."

"And you are. We got you back here, and you'll be just fine," he said, "and so will she. Right now, all we need to do is give her a chance to sleep."

Veni groaned and laid her head back against the seat and closed her eyes, but her head kept rolling from side to side with the turbulence. Finally he nudged her gently and whispered, "Come on. You can get a little closer than that."

She half smiled at him and curled up against him, his arm around her shoulders, then let her eyelids drift closed. "You sure she'll be okay?" she asked, this time barely a whisper.

"I'm sure."

Something in his tone she didn't quite like though. She didn't recognize it, didn't know what it meant, but there was just that … tone. She lifted her head to face him. "Do you think we're being followed?"

"Followed? No, not necessarily," he replied, a bit too carefully for her taste. "A little hard to do when we're up in the air, but are we being tracked? Absolutely."

She stared at him in horror, holding out her arms. "Do you think they put trackers on us?"

He shrugged. "We've checked your mom, but we haven't done a full check on you, and we probably should," he admitted. "Mostly the doctor's check on your mom made me realize that it was possible, particularly when you both were sleeping so much, while captive."

She winced. "Of course that would allow them to figure out what we were up to at every step."

"Exactly. I suspect that could also be why you were struggling to get messages out."

She frowned at him. "I didn't even consider that," she admitted. "I was thinking it was the drugs, or the place where we were being held. I … I …" She stopped, completely flummoxed. "Why wouldn't I have thought of that?"

"Because it's not what you do," he stated calmly. "You're not expected to know all the nuances of this kind of nightmare. Why would you? You live on the other side of the veil."

"And yet now I don't have a choice, since I'm on this side."

"But you don't have to stay here. You can have a nice calm, peaceful life, once this nightmare is over."

"Can I though?" she argued. "My mom is pretty insistent that I work with her and that I do the work that she wants me to do." At that, he turned to her, his gaze sharp. She shrugged. "It's about the only thing we've ever fought about."

"She believes pretty strongly in what she's doing, doesn't she?"

"Absolutely. And I … I know why. I get it. Obviously a tremendous amount of science can be developed, if we can get the stem cells that she's working with to accept healing energy. However, it's not just stem cells. It's all kind of cells …"

"As in, *everything* that lives has cells," he interrupted, thinking of the implications, truly understanding the stakes now.

She nodded. "Then potentially her work could move forward at a much faster pace."

"Sure, but at what cost?"

"That is where the problem comes in," she said, with a wry look in his direction. "Not everybody particularly cares about that aspect."

"Yet they should. She's your mother."

"Yeah, but she's also a very dedicated scientist," she noted. "I have never *not* known who my mother was. Still, I love her dearly, and she's been the best person ever in my world."

He nodded. "We'll talk to her about it all, when and if we ever get out of the air. We're on our third plane, and I'm feeling a little stir-crazy myself," he shared, with a small smile in her direction.

She nodded. "I need a shower. I need food. … Yet I know I insisted that we continue on the trip as fast as we could, and that was mostly my panic speaking."

"It was also the best answer in terms of our own ability to get you both to safety," Reid noted. "So none of us were arguing. You can have a shower in a little bit. That's hardly the be all and end all of your world right now."

She laughed. "You're just lucky I'm not high maintenance."

He flashed her a bright grin. "High maintenance doesn't really cut it in this field." He chuckled. "You are what you have always been, … *you.*"

"Why did we lose touch?" she asked, looking up at him, with a frown.

"Because I would continue in this field, and you didn't want anything to do with it."

"Yeah, that didn't work out so well though, did it?" she asked, shaking her head. "I mean, seriously look at how it didn't work out."

"Maybe, yet you needed to go your own route, maybe develop what you could do, so you would know and are at peace with your decisions, then move on from there," he suggested. "You didn't want anything to do with this before. I'm sure this captivity nightmare has affected you in some ways, and I'm certainly not trying to push you into anything. However, if you have abilities that you can develop, then maybe you should reconsider."

She gave him a blank look for a moment, and then he smiled, tucked her head closer, and added, "But you don't have to decide anything right now. Maybe down the road—and only if you want to."

"It would allow me to keep working with my mother," she conceded, yawning.

"But that doesn't seem to be your calling either."

She shook her head. "No, it isn't, and yet I don't know what I really want."

"You have time to figure it out."

She snuggled in closer and whispered, "I forgot how nice you were." She caught his wince and chuckled. "It always amazes me how people don't like to be told they're nice."

"Guys don't like to be described as nice," he clarified, flashing her a wicked grin. "We prefer *ravishing, devastating, handsome,* even *cute,* but *nice?* ... I don't know."

She looked at him strangely and said, "But nice is what absolutely everybody really wants."

"Maybe," he acknowledged. "And yet, in order to *find* nice, maybe people need to *be* nice, and I see much less of that in the world."

"That's because of the world that you're living in," she pointed out. "It never even occurred to me when I was calling out for you that you would be doing this," she shared, with a wave of her hand. "Yet apparently it's what you do now."

He nodded. "It's exactly what I do now, and I've been in it for quite a while. Once I realized what I could do, I … I couldn't let it go. I had to develop it more and more, but still … I struggled."

"Interesting, but you were very gifted."

"Maybe, yet apparently, from what I've read and heard, people do better when they're not alone at it."

She frowned at him. "What difference would it make?'

"Something to do with a ground, something to do with that extra boost of power when you need it." He shrugged. "It's one of the reasons why I will work with Terk after this."

"Right," she said, "that interesting person you keep talking about."

"Exactly. I thought maybe you'd already spoken with him."

She straightened up and looked at him. "When would I have done that?" she asked in amazement.

"I wondered if he was the person you talked to in your head that one day, but Terk said it wasn't him."

"I'm starting to wonder if maybe … I was completely off my rocker."

He smiled. "Even if you were, that stress alone would have been enough reason to break the barriers the way you did."

She slumped back against him. "But it does certainly bear thinking about, if I can talk to somebody else like this," she said. "Yet my biggest concern is that it's not somebody I *want* to be talking to."

He just nodded and didn't say anything.

She sighed. "You used to do the same thing when we were in college."

He looked at her in surprise. "Same thing?"

"Yeah, you would just give me that look, as if to say that I would work it out on my own eventually."

He burst out laughing, getting glances from the others on the plane.

Veni sighed. "I was always the butt of the jokes."

"Good Lord, how could you possibly have felt that way?"

"I don't know. It just seemed that way," she muttered. "Don't forget. At that time I was dealing with parents who were having a lot of issues. I was young and lashing out more than I needed to," she admitted, thinking back. "College was a pretty wild stage for me."

"I remember that you were definitely into enjoying it. I never really enjoyed college quite as much as you did."

"And yet it wasn't so much that I was enjoying college itself, as much as it was getting me away from my stressful home life," she clarified. "My parents hadn't come to a full divorce at that point in time. Even now I'm not sure whether they have done the paperwork to legally dissolve the marriage or will just stay separated forever. I ended up with my mother because you have to live with somebody, until you are on your own," she said in misery. "And that's another problem with the divorce. Which parent the kids choose to live with is usually the one they're closest to, yet they always feel like they're betraying the other parent. There's just no winning in a divorce."

"Depends on how the family handles it, I think," he suggested. "Granted, there are good and bad choices, but not making choices can sometimes be worse."

She couldn't agree more. "The end result was that I didn't have much of a decent relationship with my father. Whether that was my fault or not, I don't know."

Just then a yawn overtook her ability to talk, and he tucked her in a gentle hug and whispered, "Forget about it for now. Just get some sleep. It will be a while before you recover, and you need to relax."

"I'm getting that impression," she muttered, "although I was hoping I would snap out of it really quickly."

"You might, but no way to know. Still, we'll get you fully checked over once we land, and that'll be an ordeal in itself. Get some sleep while you can."

She winced. "We could just skip that part."

"Nope, we can't," he declared. "We have to ensure that you didn't come home with anything that shouldn't be there."

She shuddered at the thought. "Thanks for stopping me from being able to sleep now for a while."

At that, he gave her another tug against his arms and reminded her, "You're safe now. I won't let anything happen to you."

And, for the first time in a long time, she believed it. She whispered, "Good, because I don't think I can take too much more of this."

"I mean it," he stated. "We'll connect with MI6 here soon, but first you need to get some sleep, so you're ready for the ordeal coming up."

"And it'll be an ordeal, won't it?"

"We must know everything that happened to you, how it happened, the people you may or may not have seen, all of it," he detailed. "And these are questions I would be asking you myself, if you weren't quite so exhausted. So take the opportunity while you have it and just crash for a bit."

She let herself physically relax and then tried to shut down her busy thoughts, once again appreciating the safety of his arms. She'd expected a rescue attempt but certainly not by him. Yet she had to admit feeling a great deal of comfort in seeing a familiar face and somebody with whom she'd had such a great connection before. That he was here and had answered her call for help made it even more important. She understood what he said about developing her skills, and maybe it was time to do something about that, but how could she do that, and her mother's work too?

Was there a way to do both?

She was not sure at this point. Knowing her mother, Veni didn't think so. Still, her heart heavy and her thoughts tumultuous, she drifted off into an exhausted sleep.

REID LOOKED OVER at the doctor, who was monitoring Veni's mother. "How is Natalia?" Reid asked.

The doctor nodded. "She's holding, just needs to sleep it off. I've run a couple scans on her, but I don't have anything as high-tech as what we have back home. We'll need to get that level of equipment just to ensure no tracker is on her."

"Of course," Reid muttered. "Let's hope there isn't. It would be nice if we could catch a break on this."

"You caught lots of breaks. You rescued both women from the Russians," the doctor noted in wonder. "That will go a long way to keeping MI6 off your back."

Reid laughed. "That's the hope." He looked over at Anders. "Will you stay in England with us?"

Anders nodded. "I will for a little bit, until we've got this wrapped up for sure. If something is still outstanding here, we need to sort it out before we get too far along," he muttered. "Levi told me to stick around for as long as I need to, and I've heard from Terk on it too. He mentioned he would appreciate the extra time from me, so I'm in England for a bit. I'll give you at least a day."

"I'll take it," Reid agreed. "Not sure what we got going on here, but Veni seems to think that she's not out of danger. At least her system hasn't calmed down yet."

"I think that's probably pretty normal too," Anders replied, as Veni slept soundly in Reid's arms. "She seems to have taken to having you here."

"I think it's more about seeing a familiar face. She'll get pretty feisty, pretty quick, particularly if we decide we'll have to keep her hidden for a while. She'll want to find her new life and jump right into it."

At that, Anders stared at him in surprise. "She doesn't realize that there's still a lot of danger in her world?"

"I'm not sure that she does," Reid stated. "At least nothing I'm hearing from her is giving me that impression. It's a concern."

Anders winced. "That would be too bad because honestly it'll be a while before she's completely free. Even then I'm not sure that complete freedom will be in the cards for either of them. If you think about it, there will be quite a hue and cry over their disappearance."

"Yep." Reid nodded. "It kind of depends on what MI6 had set up for them in the first place, and that should kick into effect, now that we've got them back again. Anyway, that's what I'm hoping, but … you and I both know *best laid plans* and all that."

Anders laughed. "Isn't that the truth," he muttered, as he stared out the window of the plane. "I do see land coming up. So, with any luck, we should be landing within another half hour, and we can get some more answers. So I'll grab twenty minutes." And, with that, he settled back, crossed his arms over his chest, and closed his eyes.

Reid wished he could do the same, but it would be hard to maintain his hold on Veni. Yet he took a few deep breaths and just let the world disappear around him in order to catch a little bit of peace and quiet for whatever was coming. No way he would leave Veni in the lurch for whatever was coming up ahead, but she had to understand that having signed up for whatever help they could get from the UK government meant that the government would want help in return.

Not everybody liked paying the piper on the other end of something like this. Plus it could very likely require that both women remain hidden for quite a while, until MI6 confirmed things were okay again, something neither Veni nor Natalia would likely be very happy about.

Reid turned his head to study her mother, to see just how Natalia was doing, but there appeared to be absolutely no change in her facial expression at all. She was out cold and had been for a long time. Reid caught the worry on the doctor's face, and the doctor didn't like anything much about this either, as if she'd been under for too long. That would be Reid's take as well.

With any luck they could get Natalia into a proper facility and run a bunch of tests and find out if anything else was going on. Reid held Veni close, as they started their descent. When they touched down, he gently woke her up, smiling at the confused look on her face, as she stared up at him.

"Yep, it's me." He chuckled. "And the circumstances have changed, but not a whole lot. We are coming in to land right now."

She shifted upright, blinking to look around, and muttered, "That's good though. This is England, right?" But her tone was uncertain, as if she still wasn't too sure as to what had happened.

"Yes, we're coming into England now," he confirmed. "So all is well."

"Maybe," she muttered, as she stared around at the lights coming up on the runway below them. "You're sure it's safe, right?"

"It is safe here at the moment," he replied. "An escort waits for us down there."

"*Great,* as if I wanted to announce our arrival to the world."

"The escort will be MI6, not exactly a public announcement," he clarified, with a note of humor.

She shot him a look and then nodded. "I know. I'm sorry. I sound very ungrateful, don't I?"

"This is as good a time as any to get your grateful hat on," he warned, "because there will be a lot of questions coming up."

"Do I get a shower and some food?" she asked again.

"You will, but maybe not as quickly as you want." Her shoulders slumped at that, and he gave her a reassuring hug. "But we'll be fighting to get you what you need. So just chill, and we'll get there."

"I'm more worried about my mother," she conceded, her gaze going to the sleeping woman. "She's been sleeping way too long."

"Maybe, but the doctors will sort that out within a few minutes."

She nodded. "Then I want to go to the hospital first."

"Oh, don't worry. That's exactly where you're going because we also have to put you through a couple tests to ensure that all is well."

"I'm fine," she stated immediately.

He shook his head. "It doesn't matter what you say. You've been held captive for several days, and people need to ensure everything is okay."

She groaned. "I really won't like this next stage, will I?"

He smiled. "You'll be fine."

She hesitated, looked at him sideways, and asked, "Will you stay with me?'

He frowned at that. "My job is to hand you over to MI6."

"*Great*," she muttered. "Like a piece of meat, *huh*?"

"I wouldn't say that," he replied gently. "That's certainly not the way I would look at it."

"No, but it's the way I'm starting to look at it," she muttered, staring away. "It would be better if you could stay with us."

"*Better*, why?" he asked.

She hesitated and then answered him. "I would feel better. I don't know these people. I don't know anything about them, and, for all I know, I'll be led right back into another trap, and I'll never get out of it this time. If you were there to help me, I'd feel a little more confident that at least someone is working for our best interests. I can't be sure that anybody else here is."

Anders studied her with interest, then asked, "Do you have any particular reason to feel like you can't trust anybody here?"

Frowning at his question, she shrugged. "Just the fact that I don't really trust anybody right now."

"I can understand that." Anders nodded, then looked at Reid. "It's up to you, if you want to make that call," Anders suggested. "You can probably make it part of the deal."

"I will," Reid decided, "and we'll see what MI6 has to say about it."

"Maybe let Terk know where we stand too," Anders added. "Terk can pull a lot of strings for you."

With that said, as soon as Veni sat up, Reid pulled out his phone and quickly sent Terk a message. **Just landed. Veni is adamant that I stay close, that she doesn't trust any of the people coming into their orbit right now.**

Terk sent back a quick message. **Understandable, so stay close.**

"My orders are to stay close," Reid told Anders and Veni.

At that, Anders grinned at them. "Easiest orders ever."

She smiled broadly. "Even if you're just doing it for my sake," she teased Reid.

"There is no *just for your sake*," he said. "You and I have been close friends, even when geography and time separated us. So, when you got into a hell of a lot of trouble, I'm happy to help any way I can."

She squeezed his hand. "Good, because I'm really not sure what's coming at me now," she murmured, her tone worried.

When the airplane door opened, two men stepped on board, their gazes assessing, and when they saw both of the women, there was clearly a certain amount of relief. For the one agent, it was almost as if a checkbox had been ticked. "Both women are here. Good. Let's go." He turned to look at Reid and Anders. "We'll take it from here."

Anders smiled. "You'll take it from here, but you'll take it with us."

The lead agent frowned. "My orders are to take them to

the hospital."

"That's great." Reid stood up. "My orders are to stay close to both of them. So I guess, we will all go to the hospital."

The lead agent obviously didn't like this situation. "We're MI6, and these women are now under our jurisdiction."

"That's nice, and I'm part of Terk's team, Guardian Security, and these women have not been released from my care," he snapped.

A standoff was happening, frozen for a long moment, until the lead agent replied, "I'll have to check with my boss."

"You do that," Reid stated. "We can wait."

He glared at him and motioned at the man who came with him. "Stand guard." With that, he turned and stepped outside.

Reid looked over at Anders, who shot him a smile. Anders whispered, "These guys will take everything from you if you give it to them," he muttered. "So don't give an inch." His tone was low enough that the other agent couldn't catch his words.

As far as Reid was concerned, this was standard protocol. Still, as long as he had orders from Terk, that's where he drew the line.

Veni squeezed his fingers intently, almost hugging him. She was so close, her nerves stretched, her own pain and stress coming to the fore.

He wrapped his arms around her. "It's fine. This is just politics."

She nodded but didn't say anything, her gaze watchful, her body tense.

He kept her close, an arm around her, waiting for the lead agent to return. When he stepped back inside the plane, he shot one look at both men and snapped, "You're to accompany us."

"We probably should have just told you to contact Jonas," Anders noted.

The lead agent nodded, yet with disgust. "Yeah, that would have helped."

Reid chuckled. "We do this all the time."

"Yeah, we do too," the agent stated, "but rarely with as much difficulty," shooting Veni an odd glance.

At that, she stiffened and glared right back at him. "If Reid isn't coming with me, I'm not going anywhere."

"He is coming, so there is no need to discuss it," he muttered.

And, with that, she smiled. Still holding his hand, she and Reid disembarked, while the doctor and Anders gently secured her mother on a gurney, ready to transport. Once on the tarmac, Veni was ushered to a nearby vehicle, but she refused to get in, not until she watched her mother get loaded into an ambulance. She turned and looked at Reid.

"It's fine," he muttered. "We're heading to the hospital now too, right behind them."

"What if we aren't?" she asked, her tone suspicious.

"I will get you to the hospital," Reid promised. "We'll check in on your mother. Don't worry."

She sighed. "Yeah, well, it seems that suspicion will be my bedfellow for a long time right now," she muttered. "It'll take a while before I learn to trust again."

"And it's never a bad idea to double-check, to ensure that everything happens the way you need it to happen," he suggested. "Your mother's care and your own well-being are paramount, so let's get you both to the hospital."

She sighed.

He finally ushered her into the back of the vehicle, and they sat here, waiting until the ambulance had secured her mother for the trip. When the ambulance proceeded to leave the tarmac, they fell into line behind it.

Anders rode in the front seat of the vehicle. He looked back at her and smiled. "Okay?"

"Better, at least," she murmured.

# CHAPTER 11

W HEN THEY ALL arrived at the hospital, Veni was escorted into a cubicle, but without Reid. She looked back at him, worried.

Reid smiled reassuringly. "I'm right here. If you need me, then all you need to do is *call*." She picked up on his emphasis on *call* right away.

She hesitated, then nodded and walked in, where a nurse awaited her. She was instructed to strip down and to get under the sheet on the bed. She stared at the nurse. "Why?"

She smiled and explained, "We need to do a full assessment."

"I'm not hurt," she said quickly.

"These are my orders, per the doctor who arrived with you."

Veni didn't like it, didn't like anything about it. She shook her head. "No, if that's the case, I'll wait until I see who is coming in to see me," she declared. "I have no need to have my clothes off."

At that, the doctor from the airplane stepped in and smiled, then explained, "We're checking for trackers. It would help us do this if you would undress."

"Can't you do a scan or something instead?" she muttered. "Why do I have to strip?"

"Is there a reason you don't want to?"

"Yes," she snapped, glaring at him. "I've already been held prisoner for way too long for me to want to be so exposed."

He seemed to accept that response and nodded. "Let me do a full check on you right now, as you are," he offered. "And, yes, we can scan for trackers, but I'm also looking for points of entry. We'll find a scanner first, and then we'll sort out the entry point."

"Fine," she muttered.

"Are you sure you don't want Reid in here?" the doctor asked.

"I *do* want Reid in here," she declared, eyeing the doctor carefully. "I never said he couldn't be in here with me."

At that, the curtain was pulled back, and Reid stepped forward. "I'm here. It's all right." She breathed a sigh of relief, reached out a hand, which he quickly grasped. "It's fine."

Now the doctor proceeded to check her over for points of entry, noting drugs, yes, but also trackers. He'd done a quick check of her overall health on the plane, but, as she had been mobile and coherent and not showing any signs of actual trauma, his initial search had been cursory at best, but this was a whole different story.

By the time he was done, she was exhausted, just from the stress, the worry, the waiting. She groaned, as she sank back down on the hospital bed. "And?"

He explained, "We're bringing in some equipment, and we'll check for trackers. I did not see any sign of point of entry big enough for a tracker on visible body parts. That's a good thing, but I can't be sure. We need to be sure."

She nodded. "That's fine. Bring in whatever you need to."

And, with that, two men stepped forward, one holding a small handheld device. She was quickly scanned top to bottom, and then they stepped back. "She's clear."

The relief that washed through her was absolutely mind-numbing. She felt the tears in the corners of her eyes, as she looked up at Reid. He smiled, leaned over, gave her gentle kiss, and said, "See? You're fine."

Her breath let out in a *whoosh*. "Thank God for that," she murmured. "Now if only the rest of this goes by just as quickly."

Just then the curtain was pulled back again, and a new person entered her vision. She glared at him. "What do you want?" she asked.

He looked at her in surprise, then over at Reid and frowned. Reid immediately frowned right back.

Veni wondered if it was a secret code between these guys or something.

"I'm Jonas, MI6."

Feeling like a heel after all they'd done for her, she nodded. "Sorry. I'm not exactly trusting anybody right now."

"I guess that's a good thing. Yet you seem to trust this one." Jonas pointed toward Reid.

Reid just shrugged.

"I knew him from before," she murmured. "Reid and I went to college together."

Jonas's eyebrows shot up at that. "Really?" He turned to face Reid and asked, "You are part of Terk's team?"

"I'm on this job for Terk, yes," he clarified.

"So you're one like Terk?" He waved his hands and asked, "One of his special men?"

Reid's lips switched.

Veni looked from one man to the other. "What does

that mean?" she asked in confusion.

"He's asking if I have abilities like Terk and like you," Reid explained, "and the answer is, yes, of course I do."

"*Of course*," Jonas repeated, with a headshake. "How the hell does he find so many gifted people?"

"You would be surprised," she murmured. "There are others."

"Are there?" Jonas asked, gazing at her intently. "Back where you were being held?"

"Not that I know of," she said hesitatingly. She looked over at Reid and caught his almost imperceptible headshake to *not* tell Jonas about the other voice in her head. "However, I'm not sure there aren't other prisoners."

He nodded. "That's interesting too." His gaze went from one to the other. "The good news is, you have been cleared health-wise. Obviously we were concerned. However, they didn't appear to physically hurt you, which is a good thing. Your mother has been heavily drugged and ..." He then added carefully, "We did find a tracker on her."

She stared at him, her eyes widening in horror. "What?"

He nodded. "It's at the base of her neck, at the hairline. "Since we did just now find one, I want the men to come back and check you again to ensure something wasn't hidden in your hair. We'll just do another quick check to confirm."

With that, the curtain was pulled back, and the same men returned, but this time, instead of a small machine, they went manually over her scalp slowly and carefully.

Then they stepped back, faced Jonas, and stated, "No, she's clean."

She didn't understand. "Why would they track my mother and not me?" she asked.

"We don't have an answer for you. All we can say is that

you're clear, so that's good news," Jonas shared. "We can get you to a hotel, where you can have a shower, can change clothes, and get some rest. We'll get you some food, as well. We must keep you confined in the hotel for a couple days, while we sort out what's going on. In your mother's case, we'll have to put on extra security for her to ensure she's safe here at the hospital." After dropping that bombshell, Jonas disappeared.

Veni looked back to find Anders standing at the curtain. His face was solemn. The frown on his face made her ask, "What's the matter?"

He replied, "That tracker is worrisome."

"Yeah, I'm not really thrilled to hear that either," she murmured. "I still don't understand why they would track my mother and not me."

"Maybe because your mother's deemed to be more valuable to them?" he suggested.

She nodded. "She's the scientist, so that's definitely possible," she said, looking back where her mother was.

"But still, let's get you to a hotel, and we can hash it out there," Reid suggested. "Are you ready to go?"

"I'm absolutely ready to go, except for the fact that my mother remains here."

"Here is where she'll stay," Reid declared, "but she'll have guards on her for extra measure. MI6 is putting more security on her."

"Sure, but a couple guards may not be enough. You don't know what these people are like."

He gave her a ghost of a smile. "Oh, I think we do," he replied ever-so-gently. "MI6 will do everything they can to protect her. They went to a lot of effort to bring you guys over here, so losing you also meant hiring yet another team to go get you. They won't take a third loss. They will protect her."

And, with that, Veni was given no choice but to be led out of the room and into another vehicle.

ONCE INSIDE THE hotel, standing at the door to their suite, Reid nudged Veni toward the open door and whispered, "Come on. Let's get into the room."

She stepped inside, with the two MI6 agents and Anders right behind them. It was a large suite and much more elegant than she had expected.

Reid looked around with approval. "You'll be quite comfortable here," he noted.

"*We* will be quite comfortable here," she snapped, glaring at him. "I know I sound cranky and miserable, but honestly I don't think I can take too much more. I need"—she shook her head—"I don't even know what I need."

"You'll get what you need now. You'll get time to relax and unwind," Reid said. "So let's just get settled."

As the two agents started to leave, Reid looked back at them and asked, "What's the protocol? She needs food, and she needs clothes."

"Clothes are on the way," one of the men replied, with a nod.

"I need a laptop too," she added, turning to look at the lead agent. "Some way to communicate with the world. I lost my phone and my laptop."

"We'll get something for you."

"I also need food, and fast, please," she muttered. "I'm getting hungry."

He gave her a ghost of a smile. "Tell us what you want, and we'll arrange it."

She looked back at Reid. "You want to take this one?" she asked. "I'm heading for the shower. That's about the only thing I can think of right now."

He nodded and spoke to the agent. "We need a selection of fruits and raw veggies. She was always a bit of a health nut," he added. "I would suggest a full-on meal, something healthy, like big Caesar or chef salads, plus four medium-rare steaks and four roasted chicken breasts. Give us a budget, and we'll order in—or we can set up a delivery."

It took a little bit to get that sorted out, but—with food ordered, snacks coming, a coffee service that should be here before the food, clothes on the way, and even their own bags just brought in—Reid turned to Anders, who'd settled in with his laptop on the nearby table. Reid sat down next to him with a *thump* and muttered, "Hope that coffee gets here fast."

Anders smiled. "Hey, as long as it's on its way, you're doing fine."

"Maybe," he muttered. "Still feels a little weird dealing with MI6 on this level."

"Get used to it. All of us do."

"Really?" he asked, looking over at him.

Anders nodded. "A couple things about MI6 that you just can't let happen is their tendency to walk all over people."

"Yeah, I can see that," Reid noted.

"But start as you mean to go on, and you'll be just fine."

"I think we're good at the moment. She's in having a shower, and that should make her feel more human when she comes out."

"That and a good meal," Anders added. "It'll still take her a bit of time to realize that at least a part of all this readjustment is over with though."

"I can understand that too," Reid replied. "I'm not sure if we have security outside or whether it's even something that needs to be considered."

"I've already tapped into the hotel camera system to ensure that we have an idea about who and what's coming down the hallway all the time."

Reid raised an eyebrow. "I gather this is the joy of working privately."

"It absolutely is," Anders confirmed. "And, before you ask, no. I didn't ask permission and don't intend to tell either," he muttered. "Still, as long as we have any suspicion that Veni's in danger, we need to know if somebody's coming."

"Oh, I'm all for it," Reid said, "but I've come from the military world, where fifteen requisitions must be filled out in order to get permission for anything. So, while I'm a bit weirded out by some of the leeway we're taking, I'm definitely fine with all of it."

Anders burst out laughing. "Yeah, well, you can leave that world behind," he stated. "It's completely different when you're private, not that we're allowed to break the law, as I am doing right now," he admitted. "This is definitely hacking without permission, but, if there's a problem, you can bet that my hacking will be something MI6 covers quite nicely because of the fact that we don't dare let anything happen to Veni. Thus we need to be on top of our game."

"Right, so, as long as it's part of a safety protocol, we can work around it."

"Exactly." Anders smiled at him. "You're getting the

hang of it. You'll be just fine."

Reid shrugged. "Maybe. It's strange to consider these things from such a different aspect," he muttered. "Yet I'm intrigued enough to continue."

"Good." Anders nodded, with a smile. "I feel like I'm showing you the ropes, but honestly you already know all this stuff. You just have to get rid of that big-boss-overlord sitting in your head."

"Yet we're doing this job for MI6, so doesn't that mean we have a big-boss-overlord after all?"

"Not if it was my job. I wouldn't let MI6 anywhere close to us," he shared, "but sometimes we must cooperate and work with them, whether we like it or not."

"I would definitely say that was the case right now," Reid declared, looking around.

"And we are cooperating," Anders quipped, flashing him a big grin. "We just don't have to tell them everything."

"Ah, the classic case of making it look as if you're cooperating, then, as soon as they're gone, do your own thing."

"Absolutely."

When a knock came on the door a little later, Anders checked his laptop screen, nodded, and said, "It's the coffee service." He pointed at his laptop, which showed a person in hotel garb, standing outside with a cart.

"How do we know that they're clear to come in?"

"We don't," Anders replied. "That'll come next."

With that, Reid went to the door, opened it, and took the cart, studying the man's face for future reference. The hotel employee just turned and walked away. Reid didn't know if that was good or bad, but, hey, this was all about making it work, whatever that took. With the coffee service inside, he shut the door and quickly poured himself and

Anders a cup.

"Did you catch any sleep on the flights?" Anders asked.

Reid shook his head. "Not enough to count."

"Neither did I," Anders shared. "We can only go for so long, so I highly suggest that we take a couple turns and catch some shut-eye."

"I'm all for that," Reid replied, with a nod. "It would be nice to see what kind of shape she's in, after her shower. As you mentioned, food will help too, but she probably has a long way to go before she can unwind enough to sleep."

"You might be surprised," Anders said. "Sometimes a shock reaction can set in, and they crash really fast. Other times it's something more, and she'll need some time for adjusting. Either way, as soon as I'm done with this coffee, I'll grab some sleep, at least an hour or two." He looked down at his watch, frowned, and corrected, "Make that two. Then you need to crash, and I'll stand watch." Anders stood, taking his coffee with him, and noted, "There are two bedrooms. I'll take the smaller one." And, with that, he was gone.

Reid sat down at the laptop, studying the hallway on-screen, checking to ensure it was all good. When he heard the water shut off in the en suite bathroom, he smiled.

Moments later she popped her head around the bathroom door and asked, "I guess no clothes are here yet, are they?"

"Not yet," he said, "but I can give you a T-shirt of mine that's clean. Otherwise there should be hotel robes lying around."

"There's a robe," she noted, coming out with it wrapped around her body. She sniffed the air and smiled. "Is that coffee?"

"It absolutely is." He chuckled as he got up to pour her a cup.

"I might feel like a human being at the end of that," she said. "Sorry. I guess I've been pretty difficult to be around."

"Not at all," he argued. "Besides, after everything you've gone through, it's okay to need time for yourself."

"I'm hoping to get that time eventually, but obviously we're not out of danger yet." She stopped at the laptop and frowned at the screen. "Is that necessary?"

"I think Anders does it as matter of course, and it is a way to be prepared," he added. "Just to keep the safety level where it needs to be."

"I guess," she muttered. "I keep thinking that we're okay, but I'm not sure we are because, if you're still tracking the movements up and down the hallway, obviously you don't have the same level of comfort that I was hoping to have."

"I'm not sure that we *don't* have the same level of comfort. I think it's better to keep an eye on it and ensure that we're clear, at least until we hear back from MI6 and Terk and Levi, plus the doctors on your mother's condition."

"*Right.* I wanted to phone the hospital, as soon as I got out of the shower."

"And you can," Reid said, "but get some coffee in you first. Clothes are coming, and so is food. For now, Anders has gone to lie down for a bit."

She frowned at Reid. "What about you? You didn't get any sleep on the way over here."

"I'll crash for a bit after he's up," he shared, with a gentle smile. "Remember? This is what we do."

"Is it really what you do? To me, it seems it's what Anders does."

Reid nodded. "Anders has been private a lot longer than I have. So he's a little more comfortable breaking the rules. I am not that far behind, though." And then he laughed. "That's not even true. I'm used to breaking rules. It's just … different now."

"How so?"

"Working for Terk is nothing like being in the government and the military—as you know from comparing your college life with your work helping your mom," he added, with a smile. "So, I'm good with it. Besides, this work is special and utilizes my gifts. No way the military would. I took this job because I knew it was you and because you needed help. Other than that, I've been healing from an injury, and now that I'm out of the military and okayed to return to work, and Terk's offered me a spot on his team, I'll take him up on it."

"So then you can travel around the world doing this all the time, helping people?" she asked, looking at him in surprise.

"Something like that, yeah."

She nodded slowly. "It must be dangerous though."

"I don't know about dangerous," he clarified. "I get the opportunity to help people. That is something I've always been geared to do."

"Yeah, you always were one of those hero types," she said, with a gentle smile.

He rolled his eyes at that. "*Right.* Along with calling me *nice,* it seems like you're all about insulting me these days," he teased.

She walked over, sat in his lap, looped her arms around his neck, and gave him a hug. "Never," she muttered. "I'm very grateful for everything you've done so far."

Reid shook his head. "I don't want to make it sound as if I don't care or that what we did was minimal, but it wasn't just me."

"Right." She reached over and picked up the cup of coffee he had poured for her, but didn't get off his lap, and he just held her close.

"How are you feeling after that shower?"

"Alive," she said. "Amazing just how much that changes everything. I knew I needed the shower because I was dirty, but I can't believe just how much better I feel emotionally."

"That's huge, absolutely huge," he said, "because I don't know what's coming toward us. So the better you're feeling, the easier it will be to handle it."

She took a sip of coffee and then relaxed against his chest.

"We could move to the couch," he suggested. "It might make you more comfortable."

"Am I too heavy?" she asked, twisting her head to look at him.

He tucked her up closer and shook his head. "Nope, definitely not. I was just being polite."

"Obviously I wasn't. I just sat down in your lap, like it was normal."

"You used to do that back in college too."

She stiffened slightly and then relaxed. "I'd forgotten that. ... It seems like so many things from back then were natural and normal, and I've just picked them back up again. Yet we're very different people now."

"I don't know about that," he murmured, loving just having her in his arms. "We were close back then too."

"I wonder why we ... I know why, but I guess I just ... Now I have to look back and think that maybe we were foolish, and we had more than we realized together."

"That doesn't mean that what we had back then can't be something we can have again now though, right?" he asked. "It's not as if there's a one-time shot, and you blew it."

She gave him a sad smile. "Are you sure?"

"I'm positive. Don't even go there."

She chuckled. "I'm glad to hear that because, having found you again, even under these circumstances, we have a connection that I don't really want to lose."

"I wasn't planning on losing it," he said. Putting her coffee cup down, he twisted her in his arms and tucked her into a deeper hug. "I just don't want you to be interested in a relationship now out of gratitude or something."

She pulled back to study him and gave him a wry look. "I guess that's what it sounds like from the way I've been talking, but honestly it's about seeing you all over again and realizing just how good we were before. Even though I remember all the reasons why we broke it off, none of them seem to even matter anymore because they were all about me," she muttered, with a headshake. "It was all about my not wanting to go in the direction you wanted to go, and, even though we had fun back then, it wasn't serious in that we didn't make long-term plans."

"No, we didn't," he agreed, "and we both had lives to live. Now that we've had a chance to see the world a little, and we've reconnected, it's interesting to know that connection between us is still there."

"Interesting?" she repeated.

"Yeah, definitely interesting."

"But I would use a *different* word," she said on a laugh. She looked up at him. "I suppose you've had lots of relationships in the meantime, *huh*?"

"Not lots," he replied cautiously. "There's been a couple. Being lonely isn't exactly easy either."

"No, it isn't," she murmured. "This world that we live in is geared for pairs, and it's absolutely lovely when you belong to one, and it's the right one. However, it sucks when you don't, and the rest of the world moves on without you."

"Did you not have relationships?" he queried.

"I did, but nothing really serious, not with my parents having so many problems. And no relationship at all in the last year, not with all the lab work," she shared. "Everything else just drifted away, and it became my mother's work and nothing else. That was the problem with everything that she wanted me to do. That was her sole focus because she had left her husband, so she worked endlessly and expected me to do so as well."

"Which was hard on you because she needed a distraction, but that didn't mean you did."

She gave him that understanding look. "See? You always got it."

He chuckled. "I'm the same person I always was. I'm not sure exactly where we're at for togetherness right now, and I think it's way too early for either of us to even go in that direction, when you've just been rescued and moved to another country. However, just to know that you're safe and that we reconnected even on a friendship level is huge."

She gave him a big hug and then slowly got off his lap and walked over to the couch, where she slumped down hard. "Now that I've had a shower," she shared, as she looked over at him, "I really need food."

"It should be here soon," He checked the laptop surveillance of the hallway cameras, and then smiled. "It's here now."

She got up, tugged the housecoat tighter around her, and watched on the screen as a large cart was pushed down the hallway toward them. "Oh, good. It's very helpful to have this setup."

"It is, and, with any luck, we can see that the food's coming and that there's no danger."

She winced at that. "Because that's what it's for, isn't it?"

"Hey, it's just a warning system," he noted. "That's all it is. Don't make it more than that."

She nodded, but tightened her robe. As a knock sounded on the door, she turned to face it. "I'm not even fully dressed, so this one's on you." She headed off to hide in the bathroom.

"Hey, they're all on me," he stated, with a word of warning. "At least until we know where we stand."

# CHAPTER 12

V ENI WATCHED AS Reid pushed the trolley inside. As soon as the door was closed, then she bounded forward eagerly. "What did you order?" she asked, lifting the lids excitedly. He laughed indulgently, and she realized that she was acting like a two-year-old. She rolled her eyes. "Sorry. It's been slim pickings in the food department in my world lately."

"Hey, no need to apologize. I understand." He motioned to the table. "Let's go sit down and enjoy a nice meal."

She followed him joyfully, as he pushed the cart toward the small table they had in the room. Looking around, she noted, "This is really a nice suite, isn't it?"

"It's certainly nicer than I thought we would be getting." Reid chuckled. "That's the good news. What I don't know is how long we'll be here."

At that, she frowned at him and then winced. "Of course. This could be very temporary."

"I'm sure it probably will be, but you will be here for at least a few days, I would think." He carefully lifted the lids off several of the dishes and put them aside.

She looked at one and said, "Chicken."

"And this one has steak," he noted, "and we ordered extra, so there would be plenty. Plus I also ordered a bunch of snacks."

"Oh, good." Then she laughed. "Did you remember that?"

"I did," he replied, with a smile. "You used to snack a lot, all the time."

"I've tried hard to stop," she muttered, "but I'm always hungry."

"In this case there's lots of food, so pick what you want."

She immediately snagged a chicken breast and a Caesar salad and one of the fresh buns. "This will have to do for a starter," she muttered.

He took a steak dish and a bun, and they sat down and quickly tucked in. She sat back after a couple bites and moaned. "I forgot what real food tastes like and how it affects you when you've been deprived," she murmured. "Oh, my God, this is so good."

"I'm glad to hear that because I'm not sure there'll be any chance of changing it," he teased.

"No need to change anything, but I feel as if we should wake up Anders, so he can come get a hot meal."

"If not for the fact that he needed the sleep, I would agree, but he does need some rest. Besides, we have a microwave here, so, if need be, he can warm up his food. He knew the food was on its way too."

"Right, so if he misses out, that's his fault, is that it?" she teased, with an eye roll.

"Hardly, there will be lots of food for him when he does get up though."

And, with that, she had to be satisfied and went back to eating. By the time she had finished her plateful, he was still working on his steak. He looked over at her and asked, "Do you need more?"

"No, I'm fine." But she continued to eye his steak. "It does look good though." He immediately cut her off a bite and held it out. "No, no, no. I'll make myself sick if I eat too much more."

"Oh, I did consider that," he noted, "but you were tanking up pretty well, so I didn't want to slow your progress."

She just smiled, then remembered her mother. She quickly looked at him and said, "We need to check in at the hospital."

"We can do that in a minute. Let me finish eating."

She waited and scarfed down another bun, while he finished off his meal. Then he pulled out his phone and called the hospital. "I need a phone too," she muttered.

"It's on the way, but you're right. We haven't got that yet."

She didn't say anything to that because she'd been making demands, and she'd gotten the shower, the hotel room, and the food, so the phone could wait.

Veni listened intently as Reid got through to the hospital and watched the smile on his face, when he nodded.

"That's good news, indeed, as long as she's sleeping. If she is even a bit better, then we'll be less worried." He disconnected with the hospital and then updated Veni. "Your mom is shifting from a drugged sleep into a more natural sleep, so they're quite positive about her chances of waking up in a few hours. Not now, but in a little bit."

"Oh, good." Veni sighed with relief. "It's always so hard to watch your family suffer."

"Of course it is, which is also why your mother was willing to do what she could to get you out of there."

"She struggled so much after she and my father separated. I know she was just so focused on her work that she didn't want to listen to anything else. It was a coping mechanism for her."

"It sounds like it," Reid agreed. "Do you think there'll be major repercussions on her work after this?"

"I don't know," Veni admitted. "She did mention something about sending her work out of the country first, so she could get it later, knowing there would be no access to any of her lab-generated findings. So it'll be whatever it is, and I can't help her with that."

"So, you don't have access to it?"

She shook her head. "No, I understand it was emailed and sent via the cloud, but where it ended up from there? I don't know."

He nodded. "I'm pretty sure MI6 will be very interested in accessing all that information."

"Of course they will." She sighed. "That's the problem when your parent ends up being valuable to other governments."

"It seems you were the reason it all came to a head though."

"Probably. I think she finally accepted that my life would never be the same if we stayed there. She didn't really believe it at first. Even now I bet she's still trying to wrap her mind around all this happening, because she didn't see it and didn't want to believe it."

"Do you think she was betrayed in terms of your escape?"

She nodded. "I know she thought so, but I didn't really understand who could have known. … Whatever plans MI6 put into place should have been secure. So the fact that we were taken so quickly just didn't make any sense."

Reid nodded but didn't say anything.

"Unless you know something about it that I don't."

He immediately shook his head. "Jonas runs a pretty tight ship, though I don't know any of the details from MI6 on your extraction."

"Right," Veni replied, "because that's not who you work for."

"No, it sure isn't." Reid gave her a gentle smile. "That will also be part of whatever agreement you and your mother set up originally."

"And *that*," she said, with an eye roll, "is something that my mother set up, totally excluding me. I don't really know that I was even part of it."

"Meaning?"

"That was her agreement with them, not mine."

"Interesting." Reid frowned. "Did she even bring up the fact that you were the one in danger?"

"I have no idea," Veni admitted. "It was part of the deal for getting her out that I had to come with her. And that was not something either of us would compromise on."

"No, of course not," he agreed. "Not if you were quickly becoming somebody the Russians were interested in. How much testing did you do with her?"

"With her? Quite a bit," she said. "But it was all … It was not on paper. I didn't really want any of it going into any scientific journals, and that was the part that we fought about. She wanted it to be published, but I didn't."

"Of course because that would bring all kinds of hell on your head."

She stared at him. "You really do understand, don't you?"

"Oh, you can bet I do," he stated. "I tried hard to develop some of my skills, but it wasn't exactly well accepted in the military. I knew about Terk at the time but just as a ghostly rumor. Ever since I came out of the military," he added, "I've managed to get more feelers out and to talk to Terk about this type of work."

"Right. What about Anders? Who does he work for?"

Reid explained about Levi's team and how they now supplied men when needed for some of Terk's jobs and how Terk also supplied information and assistance for any of Levi's projects, as needed.

"It's nice to think that the world can cooperate to that extent," Veni said. "I didn't know companies like that were out there."

"And there are more like them. Anders was telling me about another one based out of Africa."

"And that's good," she said, "because the world's a mess. So the more people who we have to help us straighten it out, the better."

"Which is also why," he replied, looking at her directly, "I'll continue working with Terk."

She thought about it, then nodded slowly. "That makes sense, doesn't it?"

"It does to me," he murmured, his gaze intent, looking to see if that would bother her.

"I'm not a child anymore." She smiled at him. "I do realize, especially now, how much the world needs people like you and Anders. So, if you're asking me if I'll have a problem with it, then the answer is no."

"And yet …"

"I know. I know." She raised her hands. "I've had a lot of time to think over my life choices." She shook her head. "All I can say is, it didn't appeal back then because I didn't see any purpose for it, but now? Obviously it's a different story."

He nodded and reached out, and she grasped his fingers and squeezed. "That doesn't mean I still want to work with my mom on this, though," she admitted.

"Then you don't have to. Don't let her push you into it."

She burst out laughing. "That might be easier said than done. My mother is many things, but when it comes to her work? ... She's very stubborn."

"I wondered where you got it from." He sent her a wicked grin.

She groaned. "Okay, I deserved that," she admitted.

"Does she have any abilities?" he asked.

"Not that I know of. No one in my family does. I think that's why it was something I wasn't really comfortable with. Of course a lot of solid negative religious influence was in my world too," she murmured. "I was raised with an awful lot of talk of the devil and stories of the battle of good and evil. Some of the stuff was pretty scary back then. That was the influence of my grandparents, I guess," she muttered, staring off in the distance. She shrugged. "It doesn't matter. I didn't update my belief system, and, when I hit adulthood, college was just ... Honestly it was an escape from the headaches at home. It was a very freeing experience."

"And all of that you don't need to apologize for," he stated. "Now, do you want to stay here, or do you want to sleep on a real bed?"

She hesitated. "I'm just tired enough, so I might need to go to bed."

"Good. That would be the best thing for you."

She frowned at him. "Doesn't mean it's what I want to do, though."

"Why not?" he asked.

"It's been nice spending time with you," she said, with a smile. "You don't realize just how off your world is until you reconnect with somebody you know, and then realize how much you missed them."

"I'm not going anywhere," he said.

"I know you say that," she replied, with a laugh, "but circumstances will quite likely take you far away."

"Maybe, but maybe not. It's up to us if we want to stay in touch or not."

"I do," she declared. "As long as you do, then I guess we can find a way to make it work out."

"I do," he confirmed. "I've thought of you a lot over the years. You were about the only person I ever knew who could do what I could do, so it got pretty lonely."

"Yet I'm the one who walked away, so I don't know why you would even want to have anything to do with me," she muttered.

"Ah, stop that. It's all good."

"I don't know," she admitted. "I'm just getting very tired and emotional."

He stood up. "Anders is sleeping in the first bedroom, so go lie down in the second one."

She sighed and looked up at him.

He shook his head. "You're thinking too much. Just go get some sleep." And, with that, he nudged her toward the bedroom, where she promptly crashed.

REID SAT BACK down at the laptop and sent off several messages, then phoned Terk and checked in.

"Any signs of distress?" Terk asked.

"No, we're here in the hotel. She took a shower, had some coffee, ate, and now she's gone to lie down. Anders is taking a couple hours, and then I'll get a couple hours myself. So far, all is well. I expect MI6 to come back with clothing, a laptop, a phone, and some basic essentials for her pretty soon. Other than that, we haven't had any update from Jonas at all."

"I've talked to Jonas," Terk shared, "and they're keeping an eye on both their disappearance and on her mother's progress at the hospital, which seems to be improving."

"That's a good thing. From what I have heard, Natalia is a fighter, and apparently she's pretty dedicated to her work."

"Yes, and that has made her such a great scientist. Although I am hearing murmurs suggesting some of her work and her breakthroughs were due more to her daughter's gifts than any of Natalia's actual research."

At that, Reid winced. "I can tell you what she told me." Then he dove right in and quickly explained the scenario.

Terk whistled. "That explains why the Russians wanted Natalia and her work, but, if Veni's not prepared to do that work anymore, it'll be hard on MI6 because they've gone to a lot of work to bring her over here. Yet, if MI6's agreement was just with Natalia and not Veni …"

"Exactly. I'm not sure that the other work her mother does isn't just as valuable. Veni refused to let her mother do any testing of her gifts under proper lab settings."

"No, of course not, but that could be what her mother is hoping for now."

"Maybe, but they'll have to work that out between them," Reid noted.

"Perfect." At that, Terk asked, "What about you?"

"I'm fine. I need some sleep, but I'm good. We've got camera views from the hallway, so we can check out anybody coming this way, and, other than that, we're in a waiting game. I'm just glad to have a chance for her to rest."

"And that resting period is very important because all the questions will start tomorrow."

"Right, she'll have to be debriefed, and that could get intense. Oh, *great*. I was thinking that she was over the worst of it, but she's not, is she?"

"Nope, not yet. MI6 will want their pound of flesh now," Terk noted, with a snort of laughter.

"I'll be sticking around to ensure they only get their pound of flesh and don't try to go for two," he muttered.

"You care, I've heard."

"Yeah? Who are you hearing that from?" he asked, his back going up instantly, thinking that Anders may have shared something.

"Oh, come on. I don't need anybody to tell me that," Terk replied. "I can sense it in your energy."

"Ah," Reid grumbled, embarrassed he'd gotten so defensive. "Yeah, we met in college, as you already know. She didn't want anything to do with this energy work, whereas I was all over it," he shared. "I didn't know about you guys and went into the military, thinking that something would be there for me, but there wasn't."

"No, there isn't," he agreed, "not unless you'd found your way into *my* division, which you didn't, and now my division is private. But there is work for you, if you want to come into our corner."

"I was thinking about it," he said. "I have to admit that it would be nice to keep growing my skills. Especially now that I know what is out there for people like us."

"If for no other reason than we're all here together, that will definitely happen here," Terk confirmed, with an assurance that Reid really appreciated. "In our environment, it's pretty impossible to *not* develop and grow. Even some people who haven't had any skills in their life are slowly gathering some."

"Interesting. So, it's really true, *huh*? When you have a group of us together, everybody develops more?"

"Absolutely. More and faster," Terk stated. "So, if you're telling me that you're interested, that's cool. I've got you on the roster."

"Yeah, but I have to finish this first," Reid replied. "I can't leave Veni like this. As much as she appears to be well-adjusted and strong, she is a bit of a mess."

"Yeah, and it's not a done deal yet anyway," Terk noted. "You stick around and ensure that she's safe, and, after that, we'll talk. So don't worry about where you're going from there. I'll have a place for you at all times." And, with that, Terk rang off, leaving Reid sitting there, a smile on his face, realizing what a gift it was to have a group of people like him, who he could work with.

The smile was still on his face when Anders stepped out of the smaller bedroom a little later, yawning and wiping the sleep from his eyes. "All's well, I presume," Anders muttered, as he came in. Checking to see if there was still some coffee, he almost chortled when there was some and it was still hot.

"Yep, doing good. How was your nap?"

"It was … solid," he replied, with a nod. "I have to admit that nothing is better than getting some real sleep to clear your head. So it's your turn now."

"I'm good with that," Reid said. "Veni's gone to sleep. Food is under the covered plates, plus a bunch of snacks are around too. We've both eaten, and I didn't wake you, thinking that sleep was probably a bigger priority for you than food."

He nodded at that. "Absolutely it was. I'll get some food now, while you go catch some sleep. Then we'll both be caught up. You look like you're doing pretty well though. Interesting conversation with the girlfriend?"

"She's hardly my girlfriend," Reid stated, with an eye roll. "But an interesting conversation with Veni? Yes, and with Terk too, honestly."

"Did he offer you full-time work?"

"Something like that. At least a place to call home and to work with his group. There's a real sense of being alone in the world when you're the only one who can do this kind of thing. It's mainly why I struggled when Veni didn't want anything to do with it because I figured we were probably the only ones within who-knows-how-much distance, and I was pretty gung-ho about it. I think she's changed her mind now."

"Strife has a way of doing that," Anders noted, "particularly after what she's been through."

"I've also been keeping an eye on the hallway, but nothing's there."

"That's what we want," Anders agreed. "*Nothing* sounds perfect. Let's hope it stays that way." And, with that, Anders nodded toward the bedrooms. "Go get yourself some sleep, while you can. Then we'll reconvene in a couple hours."

And, with that, Reid headed into the spare room, but Anders suggested, "You may want to go in the other bedroom."

"Why is that?" he asked, frowning.

"Veni's not sleeping well at all. I'm guessing, if you sack

out beside her, chances are, she'll calm down and get some rest."

Reid walked into the other room to see her twisting in the bed, her arms curled up tightly against her chest. He winced and headed to her side and gently held her. "It's all right," he whispered. "It'll be fine." She opened her eyes and stared up at him, bleary-eyed and groggy. He smiled. "Sorry, I didn't want to wake you, but you were having a nightmare."

She shuddered. "Yeah, I'm not surprised. I'll probably have those for quite a while."

"Yet they will get better. They will get easier," he stated. She yawned and he added, "If you'll be okay, I'm heading to lie down myself."

"Then lie down right here," she said. "Then I don't have to worry about where you are, and you don't have to worry about me."

When he hesitated, she asked, "What's the matter? I'm hardly in any condition to take advantage of you in your sleep."

He burst out laughing. "Hey, just for the record, I'm up for that anytime. Just give me a heads-up. That's absolutely no problem." He winked at her, as he grinned happily.

She flashed him a big smile. "That was the other thing I remember about you," she said. "You always had a bright smile on your face, and nothing ever really got you down."

"Oh, things get me down," he corrected, "but it's amazing what a person can deal with in life, especially if they choose to have a good attitude."

She scooched over on the bed. "Lie down. You need some sleep, and this is the best place to get it."

He stretched out beside her and whispered, "Now you

go back to sleep."

She rolled over, so she could pick up his hand, and, with that held against her chest, she drifted off to sleep while he watched. He didn't remember her ever having that innocence, that ability to just drop into this kind of peaceful sleep, but he was grateful for it, and it made his job a lot easier too.

His own eyelids slowly drifted closed, as he headed into dreamland himself.

# CHAPTER 13

V ENI WOKE UP slowly.

She didn't think she had been asleep for very long, but, with Reid still sound asleep beside her, she shifted gently out of bed and crept into the living room, pulling the robe tighter around her. As she got closer to the bedroom door, she heard voices. Stepping into the living room, she saw one of the government men who had been here earlier, now talking with Anders.

Anders looked over at her and smiled. "Hey, they brought you some clothes." He pointed to a bag on the floor, right beside her door.

She beamed at the clean-cut agent, standing beside Anders. "Thank you." She quickly grabbed it and returned to her bedroom. Opening it quietly, so as not to wake up Reid, she found a couple outfits of casual clothing. She took them into the bathroom and checked them out—leggings, T-shirts, and a big oversized sweatshirt, some underpants, and even a bra. She looked at it hesitantly but put it on, surprised to find that it fit.

Amazed at that, and a little daunted to think that somebody could have known her bra size, she felt violated. How the hell did that work? Yet, putting it out of her thoughts, she immediately got dressed. Finding a hairbrush in her bag, she brushed her hair and quickly pulled it into a braid. She almost squealed when she found a toothbrush and tooth-paste. She happily brushed her teeth for the first time in days. Feeling almost normal now, she stepped out into the living room to see Anders looking at her critically, and then he laughed.

"Dressed like that, with your hair pulled back, you look like a teenager."

She shook her head. "It's been a while since I saw those years," she admitted, still beaming. "However, you can't even upset me because I'm dressed in clean clothes, and I feel pretty special right now." She looked around and asked, "Where did the agent go?"

"He's gone," Anders noted, "and I just ordered fresh coffee, if you're up for a cup."

"Oh, I am so ready for coffee," she said. "When's it coming?"

He pointed at the carafe, and she murmured, "Wow. You guys are pretty efficient at getting what you want."

"Sometimes we have to be," he replied, with a smile. "Come get some coffee."

She walked over and poured herself a cup, smiling at the joy of doing something normal again. "Just even getting dressed in clean clothes is … a simple thing, but …"

"It's simple, but it's also psychologically very significant," Anders stated. "It's all good."

She nodded. "Have you talked to the hospital at all?" she asked hesitantly. "Does anybody know how my mom is?"

"I spoke with the agent about it, when he was here. Your mom is starting to wake up, and it seems, in another couple hours, we can talk to her."

Her heart was overwhelmed with relief. "Thank God for that," she said happily, as she sank down with the hot cup of coffee, smiling at the world. "Now it sounds as if we're getting back to normal."

At that, he just smiled and walked over to the laptop, something coming over his face.

"What's the matter?" she asked, slowly getting up, fear on her face.

"We have visitors," he replied, "and it's not anyone who's acting like they belong here."

She raced to his side, spilling the coffee in the process. When she stared down at the face on the camera, she let out a hoarse cry. "I saw that one guy before. He was with the kidnappers."

"That's the message I'm getting too," he said, as he stared at the man's actions.

"Oh my God." She looked around in a panic. "What will we do?"

He raised his eyebrows. "We won't do anything. They are trying to find us. I have no intention of their getting in that door."

"Yes, but look," she whispered in horror, and, sure enough, he'd pulled out a handgun and was aiming it at the door.

He spoke in a calm whisper, "Get into the bedroom. Go to Reid."

As she raced to Reid, he was already bolting to his feet, almost with an inner sense, staring at her. "What happened?" he asked harshly.

"Two gunmen are here, one who I saw with my kidnappers. I think he was in the first safe house they stashed us in. He's at the door."

Reid nodded, pointing deeper into the bedroom. "Stay here. Better yet, hunker down in the bathtub."

As he raced past her, she asked, "Where are you going?"

He just repeated, "Stay in this room," then disappeared from sight.

She heard gunfire but had no idea what had happened. When no further sounds came, she slowly crept to the bedroom door, opened it a bit, and looked out. She couldn't see anything from that angle. She heard no voices; she saw nothing. She shifted to see better and saw both Reid and Anders standing, waiting at either side of the door, both with handguns—handguns she hadn't even seen before.

Just when she went to say something, another short burst of gunfire came, and the door flew open, as two men barreled inside.

She slapped a hand over her mouth and jumped back into the bedroom. She didn't want to watch, yet she wanted to do something to help. These gunmen were armed, and fear gripped her.

Hearing Reid's voice in her head, she came to her senses.

*Lock yourself in the bathroom and remain there. Get down in the bathtub and stay low.*

She bolted into the small bathroom attached to the bedroom and locked the door. And, with that done, she laid flat in the bathtub, her hands clapped over her ears, so she couldn't hear the fight going on outside. With tears running down her face, screaming for Reid in her head, she waited.

Then all of a sudden there was nothing but silence.

REID MOVED SWIFTLY, as he quickly disarmed his attacker, only to have the man turn on him and use martial arts against his own skills. The fight was hard, fast, and Reid took several ugly blows. However, by the time he stood—heaving, his chest in agony from a kick that he'd taken directly—he turned to help Anders, now standing and breathing just as hard, both dizzy. Still, they were better off than their adversaries, who were both out cold at their feet.

"Good God," Anders muttered.

"Yeah, we need to deal with this and fast. Then we have to get her the hell out of here. It'll be known fairly quickly that this job didn't work out."

With that, Anders nodded, then bent down, checked both men, relieved them of their weapons, and gave them each a hard right to the jaw to keep them down. "Let's go."

Reid raced into the bedroom, calling out, "Veni, are you there?" She peered around the corner of the bedroom. "Grab your stuff. You've got less than a minute. Let's go."

She stared at him blankly for a moment, and he noted she was still in shock. He raced into the bedroom, quickly gathering up the little bit they had, even as Anders collected the laptop and anything else personal in the living room. They were out the door and in the hallway within seconds.

As they headed to the stairs, she asked, "Are we going up or down?"

"Down," Reid stated immediately.

At that, Anders nodded. "No place to go, if we get cornered on the rooftop."

"Ouch," she muttered, as she struggled to keep up with them. "What happened to the gunmen?"

"We disarmed them," Reid stated in a succinct tone.

She winced at that. "Are they dead?"

"No, but they'll probably wish they were when they wake up. They won't feel very well."

"Good," she declared. "A part of me wishes they were

dead. I've been to hell and back, and this needs to stop."

"I agree. It does need to stop, but we're not there yet."

"What about my mother?" she cried out, freezing in her tracks.

"We'll find out when we get to safety," Reid told her, pulling her close behind him. "We'll get out a message."

"I'm on it," Anders said, from behind him. They quickly raced to the ground floor, took the back exit, and ended up in a loading zone.

"This will do," Reid muttered, as he turned to Anders. "Do you want to pick out a vehicle?"

"Yeah," he said, with a smirk. "We've got one coming in right now." He pointed to what looked like a government rig.

"Did you call them?" Reid asked.

"Nope," he snapped, his tone terse. "So either it may be a coincidence, or they're not here for us."

They watched as two men got out of the vehicle. Not liking the look of anything about this, Reid immediately backed up a bit. "I don't trust it."

"No, I don't either," Anders muttered, "but, hey, we can always take their vehicle."

As the two men raced into the stairwell, heading upstairs, the three of them headed for the vacant government vehicle. Reid handed Veni off to Anders, while he quickly opened the back door to the vehicle.

Moments later, the other doors were unlocked, and Veni and Anders climbed in, while Reid hot-wired the vehicle and disengaged the GPS and started it up.

"That's what an ill-spent youth does for you," Anders quipped.

She snorted from the back. "You were always good at

this kind of stuff. I think it's that whole energy thing again."

"Maybe. I used to play with that a lot, didn't I?"

"You sure did," she muttered.

Anders looked from one to the other. "Wait, are you saying that, with energy, you can open this kind of shit?"

"Yes," Reid confirmed. "Well, it makes it easier anyway." With that, Reid quickly pulled out of the underground parking area. "We have to get the hell away from here to somewhere safe," he said. "You want to find me a place?"

"Yeah, I'm on it," Anders replied. "Rather, Terk is."

"Okay, good, then we need to figure out who the hell those gunmen were and identify the government men as well."

"If they even *were* government men," she added, from behind Reid. "Just because they were driving this rig doesn't make them MI6."

"No, it sure doesn't, and I don't trust anybody right now. So we'll go with the idea that they were not there for the good of us, and leave it up to MI6 to track them down."

He drove around the city for ten minutes to ensure nobody was behind him and then pulled into a large shopping center and parked. "No point in driving around in a stolen vehicle until we have a location of a safe house," he explained, then turned to her. "Do you need anything?"

She stared at him blankly, then started to come out of it.

He smiled and tried again. "Food, coffee, something?"

She nodded. "Coffee would be lovely. And there's a drive-through right over there." She pointed.

"Let's change vehicles first," Reid suggested, glancing at Anders, who just nodded and jumped out. Once settled into their new ride, Reid followed Anders, as he drove the government vehicle and hid it as best he could in the nearby brush. Even with the GPS disengaged, maybe there was a second unit onboard. Either way they didn't want this rig found too quickly.

Now all in their newest stolen vehicle, Reid headed in the direction of the drive-through.

As they pulled out of the drive-through with hot coffee in their hands, Anders said, "Okay, I'm entering an address that Terk sent." After that, it took them twenty minutes to drive to the location. As they reached their target address, Reid drove on past it, then came back around and studied it. He looked over at Anders, who nodded.

"It looks fine to me. For the moment anyway," he muttered.

While Reid parked their vehicle around back, Anders took care of accessing keys to the unit. Then Reid and Veni joined Anders, as he unlocked a door on the main floor, but at the back of the building.

"So what's this?" she asked Reid in a low tone. "An easy access out?"

"Absolutely. Wouldn't you want that?" Reid asked her, as Anders unlocked the door and let them in.

She didn't say anything to that, but Reid knew, once the shock wore off, she would have plenty to say. Hell, he had plenty to say himself. As they got inside, and everybody slowly sank down into a chair, they stared at each other, wordless.

She was the first to say it. "How did they find us?"

Reid looked over at Anders. "That's the million-dollar question, isn't it?"

"It always is. We have to figure that out before we know how to get safe again."

"Obviously still some people are after you and potentially after your mother."

She paled at that, and Reid held up a hand. "I've already alerted everybody, and there's been no attack on your mother. They are prepared for it, if it comes," he added, "and they've already got more security onsite."

"I thought we were safe where we were too," Veni muttered. "That didn't seem to do anything for us."

"Not true," Reid clarified, with a ghost of a smile. "It gave us a breather, and now we know that we're still not out of danger, and that's what we need to focus on next."

Resigned, she sipped her coffee.

The fatigue on her face from the adrenaline rush hurt him more than anything else. "It will be okay, you know?"

She looked over at him blankly and nodded.

He winced because it was the nod of someone who didn't really understand the repercussions of everything that had gone on, and shock could be like that. He glanced back at Anders to find him on the phone. When he ended the call, Reid asked, "Anything?"

"They're running through facial recognition right now," Anders shared. "I uploaded photos of the two gunmen, while you were driving, so hopefully we'll figure out who they are. I didn't get photos of the people who drove the government vehicle. However, maybe they were coming to help us," Anders conceded.

"No," she snapped. "They didn't look like that at all."

"Unless the first two triggered some sort of early alert system that MI6 had set up that we didn't know about," Reid reminded her. "They could have been coming to our assistance."

She sank back and stared at him. "It's really hard to sort out who are the good guys in these scenarios, isn't it?"

"We had hoped it wouldn't be such a hardship over here," Reid admitted. "I mean, we've got you back to your homeland. So you would think that, at some point in time, the Russians would give it up."

She shuddered. "What if they don't?" she cried out. "Dear God, is this what my life will be like? Flying bullets and car chases? Damn."

"No, it won't be," Reid argued. "At some point it all has to go away. I just don't know what it'll take to make that happen."

She didn't say anything and just sipped her coffee.

He walked over and sat down beside her, then reached out a hand. She immediately took it and whispered, "It really will end one day, won't it?"

"It will," he promised. "It really will."

He didn't know if she believed him.

# CHAPTER 14

V ENI WAS SCARED to do anything right now, afraid that there would be another need to jump up and race out the door. She sat here, huddled in the chair, her feet tucked under her, her coffee long gone. As she waited for them to sort out what was their next move, she still struggled to get the shock of the attack out of her system. She was still waiting for everything to calm down, just so she could function properly. Without that, it would be even harder to carry on in the future. Everything was just piling atop each other. PTSD anyone?

As she sat there, she went through some slow, deep-breathing exercises to try to regain a certain sense of calm. At one point Reid looked over at her with approval, and she shrugged. "I'm just trying to find a way to deal."

"That's all any of us can do," he said, "and we appreciate it."

She smiled. "You guys handled that so effectively, but I'm … I'm still reeling from it."

"From what? The fact that it happened or the fact that we dealt with it?"

"Honestly? Both," she admitted, trying to keep her body from shaking. "I've never seen that kind of violence, not until this whole kidnapping thing," she murmured. "Now it seems as if my life is nothing but violence."

"We would do anything we could to not have it be that way, but, until you're safe, the reality is, there could be more of it."

Grim, she nodded. "Will we stay here for a while?"

"A little while anyway," Reid replied.

Anders nodded. "We're on the ground floor, and I'm mapping out exits right now, just in case we need it. You can never be too sure just who's after you and when they will come."

"Right," she muttered. "I mean, after all, that would be almost like knowing ahead of time that you had friends. Or enemies."

"Which we do know you have, so, in this case, better to keep an eye on our enemies."

At that, she groaned. "Is there any way to track who may have come in through the airports? I mean, there were an awful lot of known Russian agents. Is MI6 tracking them?"

"Absolutely," Reid declared. "I haven't asked who or how many may have come through in the last little while. I'm not sure that information is helpful for us because, if we can't track them, we can't pinpoint their presence. However, we're not alone in this. A bunch of other people on our teams are also working on those angles."

At that, Veni sagged back again. "I never did get a phone or the laptop that I asked for," she said angrily. "I feel so disconnected from the world right now."

"The world is still out there, and I can't say it's doing any better than it was the last time you looked," Reid quipped, with a smirk, "except for the fact that we are on this."

"And if you weren't," she muttered, a mild hysteria building, "I would be dead right now." The shock was starting to veer off.

"No, not dead, but you would be a captive again," Reid clarified. "And, if they got you back to Russia, we would definitely have a hard time getting you away from them again."

"Which would be almost worse than death," she muttered. "I wish there was a way to tell them that I can't do what my mother was so busy telling them I could—some way to just make them go away forever."

"Now that you're on their radar, chances are, they'll be looking for you for a long time," Reid acknowledged. "So finding a place to hole up and to live a life where you're safe will be paramount."

She winced. "Yeah, that won't be very easy, will it? They have long arms that stretch clear across the globe."

"True enough, so maybe being close to people who are like you would help."

She stared at him in surprise. "That sounds like you're talking about Terk again."

"I'm not sure it's even an option," Reid clarified, "because Terk has a very large and powerful group already. I'm not sure that's where either of us belongs."

"Why not?" she asked, with a shrug. "It's really hard to know what belongs where anymore."

"I won't argue with that," Reid said, "but we can figure it out down the road."

She nodded. "Of course. Besides, we also haven't been invited to his place."

"I have been," Reid shared, "but I still have to talk to him about it."

"Of course you have. You're an incredibly talented psychic, and he knows it. Me, on the other hand, not so much."

He smiled at her. "My talents are amped up when I'm with my ground."

She chuckled. "That's what you used to call me all the time, wasn't it?"

"That's because I'm pretty sure that's what you are."

"I don't understand. What does that even mean?"

"It means that everybody's energy is stronger when they're with somebody else who can help stabilize it and ground them in this plane. That much I did learn. Not that it's necessarily anything that's helpful, but I think that, for some people, a ground amplifies their energy and their abilities."

"In that case, you should have a ground."

"Oh, I agree," he concurred, amusement in his tone. "But *my* ground didn't want to do what I wanted to do." His tone was mild, but clearly something was on his mind.

She winced at that. "Yeah, well, turns out your ground was foolish." He burst out laughing, and she grinned at him. "It's a good thing we can laugh about it now because, at the time, I didn't really see anything to this. I get it now. I mean, I wasn't very forward-thinking about what could and could not happen," she shared, looking at anything but him. "Obviously my world has changed. I still don't know that this is where I want to be and what I want to do."

"Of course not," Reid agreed. "You haven't really had a chance yet to see what other energy workers can do, and it feels like everybody is trying to force you into something that you don't want to do. What I think is important, right now, is for you to decide what you want to do and then see if you can make it happen."

His words were prophetic in many ways but also difficult because how did she figure out what she wanted to do when things were such a mess? She could do many things, yet nothing really appealed. She knew her mother was fairly aggressive about wanting Veni to work in the lab with her, but how did Veni get it through to her mother that she wasn't interested? No matter what her mother thought of it, Veni didn't want to invest her life in that work. How could she get it through in such a way that her mother didn't end up hating her for all time, since her own life's work would potentially move forward at lightning speed, if only her daughter would help?

*Why is it that I* don't *want to help Mom?* she asked herself.

She pondered that question for a long moment, as the men discussed the circumstances around them. All she could really come up with was that she wasn't really against helping her mother, but Veni was dead set against being locked into doing only that. An awful lot of other things were out there that she would like to try or experience, and she definitely didn't share her mother's intense focus on nothing else but her work.

The problem was, it was her mother's work, and it wasn't Veni's work. She would love to know what else she could do on that level, but she wanted to do it in a safe environment, not where she was a prisoner, and not where she was told what she could and couldn't do. That just didn't appeal to her in any way. But would her mother ever listen? *That* Veni didn't know. Her mother surely hadn't so far. Her mother had a mind of her own when it came to this kind of stuff, and that made it more difficult to figure out what Veni might be up to herself down the road.

If her mom could just continue on this pathway, and Veni could stop in and do some work every once in a while, that would be fine. However, she didn't think that would be enough to satisfy her mother. She had this thing about ordering Veni around. Like, *increase the energy now, change the intensity, affect these cells here, put some energy over there,* and it just went on and on.

Veni hated to say it, but a large part of what she disliked about the work was the forced dedication that her mother insisted on and that Veni continue with her mother's work. If her mother had any understanding that it wasn't what Veni wanted to do and then accepted it, it would be a whole lot easier to help her mother sometimes. But there was no *sometimes* where her mother was concerned; it was *all the time.* Veni suddenly realized that was probably why her parents' marriage had failed. Maybe it hadn't been her father's incredibly intense focus on his work. Maybe it was the both of them.

That thought was exhilarating. The fact that they were both just as crazy about their scientific endeavors and their research and their work and their results meant that they were also well-suited in many ways and complemented each other in other ways. Yet otherwise they were completely unsuited because neither of them was prepared to look beyond their own needs to consider what the other needed.

As Veni saw how her mother was at work now, Veni wasn't at all surprised that the marriage was no longer something either of them were interested in continuing.

It made her sad, but, considering how absolutely stringent and dedicated her mother was, maybe it was for the best for all of them.

REID NUDGED ANDERS gently and signaled him to keep his voice down.

Anders was on the phone and was getting louder, and Reid wanted Veni to keep sleeping.

Anders took one look around, then nodded, as he ended the call. "Sorry."

"It's all right. I didn't expect her to fall asleep so fast, but she's obviously exhausted."

"With good reason. The shock, the adrenaline rush, and she's still not recovered from being held captive. At least this way she'll be ready, if we have to make another run for it."

"I'm really hoping we don't. That kind of shock is rough on her."

"It is, but we have to be ready regardless."

"Yeah, I know." He left his tone open-ended on that because Anders was right. If that was what they had to do, they would do it. They would up and run again. But, in order for that to happen, they had to have some new bolt-holes where they could run to.

A few minutes later, Anders was back on the phone, but he had lowered his voice and had carried on the conversation at more muted tones. Reid got up, went into the bedroom, and came out with a blanket, which he gently put around her shoulders.

She would be a lot more comfortable if she would go into the bedroom and sleep, but she had refused that earlier, not wanting to be in the same position she'd been in the last place, separated from them. Even though it was a matter of a few minutes difference at best, she was not prepared for that again. He understood it, but she wouldn't rest well like this. He contemplated picking her up and moving her to a more comfortable bed but ended up deciding against it. As long as she was sleeping, he would leave her be. The problem was, she very quickly started tossing and turning in the chair, and he was afraid she would end up falling off.

He gently picked her up. Instinctively her arms went around his neck and held on. He carried her into the bedroom, knowing that, even though that's not what she wanted, it was probably what she needed. He just laid her on the bed, but she wouldn't let go of his neck. Shifting to lay her down and to also lay down beside her, he just held her close and waited until she relaxed into a deep sleep.

As soon as her arms relaxed, and she no longer held on to him, he grabbed a blanket, pulled it up over her, and rubbed her shoulders gently to ease her back to sleep. He looked up to see Anders standing at the doorway, watching him. Reid got up and headed to the door. "I figured she would get some better sleep this way."

Anders nodded. "It's definitely better for her in here, but she may not appreciate it when she wakes up."

Reid grimaced. "I know. She's likely to be pretty stressed when she wakes up and finds herself in yet another new room, but we won't be far away." He looked over at Anders. "Anything yet?"

"They've run the hotel video cameras and have a facial recognition on one gunman but not the other. They figure one was locally hired help because he has a record here in England, mostly petty stuff. So they probably hired somebody small-time just for the job."

"This wasn't exactly petty stuff, and they came in well-armed and skilled," Reid pointed out.

"That's why they think somebody is behind this group as well, which probably means they're just trying to put distance between them and the job."

"Right. And the two so-called government guys?" Reid asked.

"Yeah, and then there's that. Seems MI6 can't ID them, but they are working on it."

Reid stared off into the distance. "It still doesn't change the fact that we need to figure out who the hell is behind doing all this and how to put a stop to it, as well as determine how they are tracking us."

Anders added, "My money is on Levi or Terk finding out who the two G-men are first."

"Yeah, me too. As far as tracking us, Russia had a tracking device buried under Natalia's hairline, which we didn't find until we got here. So that brought the Russian right to England. And the Russians knew we would check out both women at a hospital most likely. We may have just a rotating shift of men on foot, tracking us the old-fashioned way, with boots on the ground."

When Anders's phone went off not a minute later, Anders answered, his frown instant, as he stared at Reid. "Seriously? No, no, I'll ... I'll get back to you soon." He disconnected and asked Reid, "Did you know her mother was sick?"

His eyebrows shot up. "What do you mean by sick?"

"Like really sick, as in cancer sick."

Reid shook his head slowly. "Oh God." He was truly shocked. "No. I don't think Veni knows that either."

"That doesn't mean the mother didn't know though."

Hearing an odd sound, Reid turned to see Veni standing in the doorway of her bedroom, rubbing the sleep out of her eyes, staring at the men in confusion. "What about my mom?"

Reid walked over to her. "Look. I don't know whether

you heard this or not, but you need to brace yourself. The phone call we just got, and we'll have to call them back again for more details, was about how your mother isn't doing as well as could be expected."

She stared at him, blinking, and then turned around in a panic. "I have to go. I have to go see her."

"Whoa, whoa, whoa, calm down," Reid said. "There's something else."

"What else can there be?" she cried out, raising both hands in frustration. "This is a nightmare."

"It's a nightmare, yes, but there is more here that we have to figure out. According to the doctors, your mother is sick, as in very sick." She blinked, and she was about to fall sideways as he caught her. Scooping her up in his arms, he walked over to the nearest chair and sat down with her in his lap. "Take a deep breath," he whispered. "Just breathe."

She stared at him with a vacant gaze, still not even processing this newest info. "I had no idea."

He nodded. "I wonder if that's why she was so adamant about doing the work."

She moaned, the tears slowly trickling from her eyes. "That would explain it, wouldn't it?" she whispered. "She wanted to ensure that she left a legacy, so that her work would live on." She shook her head, the tears coming faster and faster. She angrily wiped away the tears, and there was a finality in her tone. "We have to go, Reid. I have to go to her now."

He expected that response, although not quite so fiercely. Still, he should have known because he knew what Veni was like. He tried to warn her, saying, "It'll be dangerous."

She waved her hand at that. "Everything has been dangerous, and I really don't give a crap. I have to get to my mother."

"Listen. I don't know that she's dying," Anders stated not-so-delicately, from the other side of the room. "I just got off the phone with the doctor. He's not sure how long she's got left to live, but it's obvious that she's had this condition for a while."

"Yet she was always so healthy," Veni argued, staring at him.

"No, she was always taking medication that kept her drive in good form, while her body slowly wasted away," he clarified. "The drugs were strong enough that she could continue to work happily, ignoring everything else going on, until she needed the next dose."

Veni shuddered at that. "Dear God," she whispered. "Why didn't she tell me?"

"She probably didn't want you to worry, but it would also explain why she wanted to make the move now, so that you weren't stuck over there after she was gone."

She blinked at him, and her face scrunched up.

Reid immediately snatched her into his arms and held her. "I'm so sorry, and, yes, we'll get you to her. I'm not quite sure *how* at the moment, but we will get you over there."

"*Now*," she declared, tossing her head back and looking at him fiercely. "I need to go now, and you can feel it too, can't you?"

He blinked and then winced because—now that the subject had been addressed, with her in his arms—he did feel it himself. Her mother was definitely slipping away. He looked over at Anders. "She's right. We need to go soon." He added, "She's not just fading. She's fading quickly."

Anders looked from one to the other and then nodded.

"Then I guess we had better just go." And, with that, he led the way to the back door and out to the vehicle. He went to the driver's side without looking back, his mind already made up. "I'll drive."

"That's good," Reid agreed, "I need to be with Veni." He opened the back door for her. Then Reid went to the passenger side of the car.

Anders nodded. "Yeah, it's a good thing you're here for her. It could get pretty rough ahead."

"It'll definitely get rough ahead," Reid noted. "Damn, why didn't I see that before?"

"Probably because the drugs were masking it. Is that possible?" Anders asked him.

"Yeah, I think it is. I can't know for sure, but that kind of fits." Both men settled in the front seat of the car.

Anders continued. "It also fits that Natalia would have kept it to herself. I don't remember hearing very much about her mother, but Veni always spoke with such admiration about her mother being such a strong woman. Of course, in this case, that strength was all about her work. She put everything she had into her work, trying to get it finished before this took her out."

"Exactly," Reid agreed, "and that's why she pushed to get Veni to help her as much as she did because, if she could get something completed and handed off, then her work wouldn't have been in vain."

And Anders agreed. "We can definitely hand off her work, but we need to get a copy of it," Anders suggested, looking at Reid.

"I don't know if there even is a copy."

Veni spoke up and said, "I think I know how to get a copy."

"Good," Reid replied. "That would be very valuable if you could, and it would also make your mother feel a whole lot better, just knowing that you can do something about making sure her work gets into safe hands."

"Can I though?" she asked, looking at them. "I mean, are we capable of making such a promise to her? We're running for our lives, for God's sake."

"I'm not so sure about that," Reid countered. "We have more resources at hand, being in England, with backing from both Levi and Terk. We are actually situated quite nicely here, with the exception of putting you in harm's way with these public appearances. Still, we understand your need to be at your mother's side. Yet are you really ready to tell her that you can't hand down her work to someone who will carry on her passion project?"

She winced. "No. God, no. She's dying, … so let her die in peace. I'll do everything I can to ensure it happens after the fact. Hell, maybe I'll take up that sword myself."

"That is," Reid clarified, "after you rethink what it is *you* want to do with your life."

# CHAPTER 15

THE DRIVE TO the hospital seemed interminable. Veni kept going through everything her mother had said over these recent months of their working so closely together. Yet it was her variable personality that should have raised red flags with Veni—her mother's violent mood swings, the fatigue that would hit her all of a sudden, and sometimes the harsh irrational need for Veni to do the work that her mother demanded that Veni do, whether it was what Veni wanted or not.

All of it just clicked into place now. It had been such a large part of the problems between the two of them, as Veni just hadn't been dedicated to the same cause as her mother. Yet now Veni found herself in a situation where her mother was no longer capable of doing this work, and all Veni could do was feel guilty. "I should have helped her more," she blurted out.

"No, you shouldn't have," Reid argued. "You still have to pace yourself, and you still aren't doing as well as you would even like. You've taken a lot of chances in these last few years with her as it is." He shook his head and then took her hand. "You're not responsible."

"I didn't help her."

"You were working in a Russian lab for the last year at least, doing nothing but your mother's work," Reid argued.

"She didn't tell you about her cancer, which means none of your decisions were based on being fully informed," he added, and she glared at him. "No, I won't let you feel guilty. Your mother was totally invested in that stem cell research, and she made the decision to pursue it, even at the peril of her own health. She must have felt this was the greatest purpose for her own soul's journey, and you cannot take that from her. However, you also cannot blame yourself for something you did not know."

She stared at him in surprise. "That was very esoteric," she muttered.

"Yet how do you know I'm wrong?" he asked right back to her. "When we look at all the things that people do and at some of the absolutely miraculous things that they do for each other, this is just another example. This is what she wanted to do. Don't take it away from her, don't make her feel guilty because she didn't tell you that she would not be around much longer. Maybe she thought this would be her own cure but then noted it wasn't working anymore. So, she needed to get you out of Russia before you couldn't get out at all. Maybe that had nothing to do with it. Maybe she thought, when she got to the Western world, there would be other medicines for her. I don't know. We don't know everything there is to know. The fact remains, as far as the doctors are concerned, it's too little, too late."

Veni winced at the bluntness of his tone. "God, the reality of it all is such a bitch."

"It can be. It absolutely can be," Reid agreed, "but it doesn't have to be your reality. Right now your mom could be in the last stages of her life, but that doesn't mean that your life has to be completely destroyed because of her choices."

"Yet they were my choices too," she cried out. "I could have helped her more. Maybe we could have found a cure sooner."

Veni knew that there was no rhyme or reason to the guilt running through her, except that she had always refused to do more, and now that she understood why her mother was so adamant, it just made Veni feel even worse. "I feel so guilty," she whispered. He reached out a hand and just gently held hers. She stared down at it saying, "Why would you even want to be with somebody like me?" she muttered. "I could have done so much more, and I didn't. At every turn, I walked away from opportunities. … I didn't even think about other people, what I could do for other people. I just didn't want to do what was right there on the table."

"Life is all about choices," Reid pointed out. "Maybe you weren't ready. Maybe it was more about rebelling against your father's never-ending mandatory rules, and, once you found freedom, it was hard for you to even want anything else. And maybe, if you knew your mother was dying months ago, then you would have gladly helped more. But now? You have to cut yourself some slack here. It won't be an easy afternoon, if we even get in and get a chance to talk to her. Still, you need to be calm and help her through whatever is coming up. Can you do that?"

She nodded immediately. "Yes, I can be there for her. She was there for me all these years. I can be there for her."

"What about your father?" Anders asked from the front seat. "Did he have anything to do with your mother's work?"

She laughed. "He tried to take credit for it. The two of them fought constantly, and he finally ended up going off and doing his own research. I don't know if it was exactly the same thing because I haven't had anything to do with him in quite a while," she shared, thinking hard, "but it was the same kind of work."

At that, the two men exchanged glances.

"What does that mean?" she asked, her tone hardening.

Reid sighed. "It means that we're wondering if he would have anything to do with this kidnapping event and if he wanted the research she's got, so he could continue his work."

She stared at him. "I don't know." She rubbed at her face. "I don't know how much between them was good and how much of it was bad. As a teen I just saw the bad. I saw and heard the fights, the anger, the constant working, the competition," she shared, with a shudder. "That was one of the worst parts. They were always fighting about who was better, who was the best, who would get the next grant. It was really very sad. It turned me away from so much in life," she admitted. "I just wanted to live a little in peace."

"You did. You went and lived a little while you went to college," Reid reminded her, "but now reality is biting you in the butt again, and decisions have to be made."

She took a deep breath. "Right. Decisions must be made, … whether I like them or not."

Reid added, "And I am wondering if he's behind the *rescue*, not so much because of you guys trying to come to England and leaving Russia, but so that Natalia's material didn't get lost with her. Her lab material, her research."

"He might have been able to hack into her databases," Veni suggested. "I don't know. That was something my mother was also incredibly protective of. She told me that my father had no scruples and that he would steal anything from anybody."

"Interesting marriage," Anders muttered from the front

seat.

"As I said, it was a nightmare. They were just so competitive with each other that there was no break, no joy to be found. They were two of a kind, which is probably what brought them together, but it's also what split them apart."

"And that can happen too," Reid noted. "I mean, there has to be give and take, and when there's just *take* and *more take*, it doesn't work."

She smiled mistily up at him. "That's partly why I sent you away. I could see your dedication to finding out more about your gift. I could see how eager you were, how passionate you were about all this." She whispered in a monotone, "It terrified me to think that you would be like my father."

He stared at her in surprise. "That hurts."

She laughed. "I was a whole lot younger then, and I wasn't looking for permanence. I was just looking for a life that wasn't the same kind of nightmare I'd been raised in," she murmured. "Of course that wasn't really helpful."

"Yet it explains a lot," Reid noted. "So I'm glad that you had a few years with your mom, with some relative peace and quiet and joy, amid what seems to be a ton of work."

"Yet, when she needed me, where was I?" she asked.

"At college, you were doing what you were doing," he stated. "Enjoying life on your own terms. Don't hold that against yourself. You deserved some peace and quiet and joy too. Then you went to work with your mom. You were doing what you could to be loyal to both of you."

It was easy for him to say, but Veni knew it would be a long time before she could come to terms with all that had happened between her and her mother. Veni could only hope that they still had some time, … a few years, something. Veni needed more time. "Do you think she's … *dying-dying?*" she asked hesitantly. "Did they say anything?"

"No, they didn't really want to talk to us at all," Anders replied from the front seat. "You are family, so they'll tell you more. Of course the government also wants to know because they helped bring you over. Along with that is the fact that they'll want something for all their efforts, and if *she*'s dying on them …"

"Then she isn't there to give it to them." Veni tried to hold back the bitterness in her tone, but both men obviously heard it. She sighed and took a moment to calm her nerves. "I'm sorry. I don't … I don't mean to be upset about that," she explained. "Obviously I am much happier here. I'm safe, or at least safer, and that's what's important. It's just frustrating to think that we're more or less safely in England now, but my mother can't live that life that she wanted to have here."

"I'm not sure it was a life *she* wanted at all," Anders suggested. "I mean, if she's as sick as we're thinking she is, that wouldn't have been what she was concerned with. I'm certain her thought processes were on you."

Veni pondered that because, although she had no illusions about her mother's drive and dedication, she also knew that her mother loved her. It's just that it was a constant war as to whether she loved Veni enough to let her do the things she wanted to do or to keep Veni as a pawn for the things her mother wanted her to do. "I just need to talk to her," she muttered.

"We're hoping we can give you that. At the moment we're not being followed, and our ETA is approximately six minutes," Anders shared. "There will be some security meeting us there, and more is at her bedside. So don't be alarmed to see more strangers around your mom, when we visit her this time."

"Right. So don't freak out when I see men with guns, *huh*? Got it."

Reid chuckled. "You've done very well so far. Just stand strong."

And again, it was easy for him to say. It wasn't his mother lying in that hospital bed, having just gone through hell to get them here. She thought back to the last conversation she'd had with her mother. "Why wouldn't she have said something about this, when we were together for maybe five minutes, while still in captivity? My God, even under those dire circumstances, she couldn't tell me?"

"Think back on what she *did* talk to you about," Reid suggested, studying her. "Maybe that viewpoint helps put it in a different light."

"It may," she replied. "I'm just not sure I fully understand."

"If you get a chance to talk to her, then maybe you can get the answers you need. Otherwise it'll be anybody's guess."

That's not what Veni wanted at all. Minutes later, the hospital loomed in front of them. As she got ready to bolt from the car, Reid grabbed her arm and said, "Easy. Hold up a minute."

He got out, checked the surroundings, then walked around to her side of the vehicle. He quickly opened the door and, keeping her body shielded from anybody else, led her inside the hospital.

"What about Anders?" she asked.

"He's coming, but he'll park the vehicle and do a quick recon. Then he'll check in with the security group here to ensure there's nothing we don't know about."

"Got it," she muttered.

She didn't really care. She didn't give a crap about anything but having a few minutes with her mom, if there were any minutes to be had. Veni hoped her mom wasn't quite gone yet and that they would have six months or even longer, if that were possible. That was something she would definitely talk to the doctors about.

As they got up to her mother's room, the doctor stood there, talking with a nurse. He looked up with relief in his expression and said, "Good, I'm glad you made it."

She froze. "Is she that close to dying?"

"I'm not sure what medication she was on. She can't tell us, but she's experiencing withdrawal symptoms. Whatever it was, it appears to have run out of her system." He took a moment to review her chart in his hand and then focused on Veni again. "Do you know anything about her medications?"

"No, I don't," she replied, staring at him blankly. "Honestly I didn't even know she was sick."

"That's what I was afraid of." The doctor pinched the bridge of his nose. "She's probably been experimenting on herself, and, whatever it was, it was working for a while to hold this at bay. Yet, in time, the crisis in her body, the devastation, has taken over, and she is declining rapidly."

"I need to see her," Veni said immediately.

"You can." He led the way to the room and let her in.

"Can I go in with her?" Reid asked.

The doctor hesitated, then looked over at Veni, but she was already at her mom's bedside. "I guess," he murmured. "God knows it's pretty sad when we finally get somebody free of the nightmare they've been in, and yet they end up dying on us anyway. I heard a lot of talk about some research she has been working on, and, if it was something keeping her disease at bay for a while, I would be interested in learning more on that. I would definitely like to see it. I just wish we had those actual lab records," he murmured. "So, if nothing else, maybe you could see if that is available. While it may not help her mother in time, it could save others' lives."

Reid nodded. "I'm aware that the government is hoping to get something out of this as well."

The doctor nodded. "They can hope all they want, but I'll be surprised if she lives through the day."

"Oh, crap," Reid muttered, staring at him in surprise. "We were hoping she had more time than that. It's been quite a shock, especially since Veni didn't even know her mother was ill."

"Nobody did, at least not until Natalia started to slide very quickly. Presuming that she had enough of the drug in her system to get her this far, then it was a case of whether she would make it or not when the drug was discontinued. I suspect she already knew all this going into it."

"That's what we're slowly realizing. Maybe throughout all these machinations, Natalia probably had her own agenda heading in, and well ..." Reid stopped and asked, "What's her diagnosis?"

"Stage four lung cancer," he replied. "No coming back from it."

"Right, *great*."

And, with that, Reid headed into the room to join Veni.

"HOW IS SHE?" Reid asked Veni.

"Not conscious," she grumbled.

"She has stage four lung cancer, according to the doctor."

Veni stiffened and then sagged. "Of course she does. She had cancer years back and beat it, but she didn't tell me that it had returned."

"No, but there could have been all kinds of reasons for that."

"I know she absolutely detested the treatment process. She told me that, if it ever came back, she didn't give a crap. She wouldn't go through the chemo and radiation again."

He didn't say anything to that. What could you say? Natalia had made a decision, and it was now obviously time to say goodbye.

"I just don't understand how she went downhill so quickly," Veni muttered.

"The doctor says that she was pretty heavily drugged, as if maybe she had her medication with her and took the last of it, knowing there was a possibility she would either make it or she wouldn't."

Veni stared at him blankly for a moment and then nodded. "I'll just sit here for a while. I'm hoping she wakes up."

"I hope so too," he agreed, as he pulled up another chair and sat down with her.

"You can go off and do whatever needs to be done," she said, waving her hand in the air.

"I could, but that *whatever* happens to be looking after you right now."

She sniffled, feeling the tears in her eyes.

"Don't you dare say I'm a nice man," he teased.

She burbled with laughter. "No, I won't say that, not now that I know how you feel about it." Then she turned and looked at him sideways. "But it's true."

He sighed. "There you go again, with the insults."

She chuckled. "You just don't like being hero material."

"*Hero material*? Now that is a whole different story, but *nice*? No, that's a friend-zone word."

"Maybe it is to you," she relented, "but the man I've seen, who's looked after me these last few days, well, he's the man I wish I hadn't let go way back when."

"We weren't ready," he repeated.

She sighed. "We were different people in a different time."

"Yeah, and apparently you didn't want somebody who was very dedicated to figuring life out—or understanding more of my gifts."

"No, apparently not," she agreed, with a headshake. "Sometimes I wonder if I had any clue who and what I was and where I even was."

"A certain amount of that is to be expected. I mean, you were young," he stated. "We were both very young and naïve, and it's not as if we can have all the answers just because we want to."

"I guess so, but it still would have been nice to know I had the answers I needed back then."

"I think we're meant to figure it out," Reid suggested.

"Veni?"

She sat up straight and reached out for her mother's hands. "Mom, you're awake. Are you okay?"

Her mother stared up at her with a smile and said, "It seems I'm in the hospital, so I guess you know about the cancer by now."

"Yes. We're in England and safe here at the hospital, but I'm just finding out that you have cancer, and you've been hiding it so well. That's not fair."

"I've been trying a chemical mix of drugs on myself for the last several months," she shared, "getting ready for the day that we could potentially get out of there. You have to protect my research," she declared, staring at her daughter, squeezing Veni's hand tightly.

"I will, Mom. I will."

"I don't want you doing the same kind of work. I can see how it ruined my life, your life, and your father's," she admitted. "Yet there are doctors who need to see what you can do."

Veni winced at that.

"I know you don't want that, but if the wrong people ever find out what you can do—"

"I know. I'll take care of it."

"What does that mean?" her mother asked, with a groan. "You never really were the kind to take care of anything."

Veni winced. "Hey, that's hardly fair. I just wanted to have a life."

"And it's a life that we didn't give you, I know," she murmured. "Only as I look back on all these wasted years do I realize there was another way to do it. I want you to find that other way, Veni. Find a way to have a life and to enjoy it, instead of always yearning for something that we couldn't give you."

"Couldn't give me?" she asked, frowning at her mom.

"*Wouldn't* give you," she corrected. "I'm just as responsible as your father."

"Is Dad after your research material?"

"Oh, he might be," she replied, "but he's light years behind us, so he's not really a worry."

"But what if he spoke to the Russian government, which

I presume he did. That was part of the impetus to getting us back there."

"He didn't know about the cancer coming back. I didn't tell anyone," she whispered. She started to cough then, and all conversation ceased, until she could clear her airways. "I'm not getting out of the hospital now either," she admitted. "Honestly I just want to be pain-free for my last little while. I thought I could make it longer. However, the relief of making it here, of getting out of that country, of keeping you safe," she explained, "now I feel that I can let go and be totally pain-free."

Veni felt a flood of emotions at her mother's words. "You're free to go anytime you need to, Mom," she whispered. "But if you can find a way to stay around a little bit longer, well, I know a young lady who would very much like to have her mother for as long as she could."

"You had her," she replied gently. "My time is done. I'm used up and worn out." She took a few deep breaths and closed her eyelids for a moment. "Don't do what I did, Veni. Don't put it all into the lab. There are other things in life. Go find a partner, have children. Know that you were the best thing I ever did, and I didn't even plan to have you," she shared. "You are the joy that I never knew I needed in my life, but you helped me. You helped me to see that there was another way."

Veni couldn't imagine that because it hadn't seemed as if there ever was another way possible with her mother.

"The thing is, I didn't see it until it was too late," her mother whispered. "Now it's not to be. And I'm okay with that too. I'll stay in the hospital where I'm safe." Her mother closed her eyes and whispered, "I'd like to rest now."

# CHAPTER 16

VENI TOOK THAT as a dismissal, which was so very like her mother. Veni got up and walked out of her mother's room, even as a nurse came in and checked on her patient.

"Good God," Veni whispered to Reid, wrapping her arms around her chest. "It's so hard to believe that she'll be gone so soon." She stared up at Reid, bewildered. "There was no warning—or no warning that I allowed myself to see," she muttered, with a wave of her hand.

"What about your father?" he asked. "Should you let him know?"

She stared up at him in confusion. "I … I don't really know. I mean, she would've called him her one great love, outside of the lab," she added, with an eye roll. "I think he probably would say the same thing."

"But he probably doesn't know that she's dying, does he?"

"I don't think so. Mom just now told me that she didn't tell anyone, including him specifically, but who knows? Funny how my supposed lie-detecting gift doesn't work with Mom. And I haven't spoken to Dad in months."

"But months, not years, right?"

She nodded. "Months, not years," she confirmed. "We did talk on an irregular basis. But they had a huge fight, and things, well, they were never the same afterward."

"Do you know what that was about?"

"I'm guessing it had to be about work, that ongoing competition between them, but I don't know what aspect it was in particular," she said. "I'm not even sure they would remember."

"Let's go get a cup of coffee. The doctor is checking on her now," he said, with a nod toward the room behind her.

She watched as the doctor checked her mother over. "Sure. I … I kind of need to clear my head."

"Coffee then. We'll come right back, and, if she's awake, we can visit some more."

"Okay, that sounds good," she muttered. She looked up at him. "Thanks for sticking around."

He wrapped an arm around her shoulders. "No thanks needed. If for no other reason, you're a longtime special friend, and you're hurting, so the least I can do is be a comfort right now."

"You've done a lot more than that," she said, "and I know you don't want me harping on it, but I am grateful. I can't imagine where I would be right now without all that you've done." With a smile she linked her fingers with his and added, "Come on. I'll let you buy me a coffee."

He gave a burst of laughter. "That's good because I could use some coffee and maybe a bite to eat too, although hospital food? … I'm not so sure about that." He cringed.

"I understand," she said, "but maybe a muffin or two."

At the cafeteria, they quickly picked out a couple muffins and ordered several coffees to go, then slowly wandered back to her mother's room.

When they got there, Veni paused outside. "I'm probably not allowed to take food in there," she muttered.

"We can sit here on the bench, if you want."

She nodded, and they made themselves comfortable for a moment.

The nurse stepped out of the room and smiled at Veni, sharing, "She's sleeping right now, but, as soon as she's awake again, you can go in and visit."

"Thank you," Veni replied. "I was wondering if I could just sit inside."

"The doctor's still with her right now," she pointed out gently. "When he's done, you can go on in." With that, the nurse left.

"I thought she said that my mother was sleeping?" she pondered.

"Or close to sleeping?" Reid suggested.

Veni shrugged. "I guess that's possible too." After a few more minutes, their muffins eaten, yet the doctor didn't come out, she hesitated, then asked him, "Is it just me?"

"No. Why isn't the doctor out yet?" He stood up and looked through the observation window. "He's sitting on the bed, talking to her."

"So, she's not asleep."

"No, although she looks very tired, as if she's just one step away from it."

"Right." She stood up and walked beside him to look in the window. Then she gasped. "Oh, my gosh." She quickly raced to the door. "That's not a doctor." She tried to open the door but found it locked. Wide-eyed, she looked at Reid. "That's my father."

REID STARED AT Veni in disbelief, then looked through the

window again. "That explains why the door is locked and why they're talking like old chums. You might also consider that he is her husband, and she's dying, so maybe give them a moment."

She frowned and looked back through the window again. "They are holding hands, aren't they?"

"They are," he agreed. "So I'm not sure what their relationship really is or whether you want to just barge in there or not, but maybe let them have their moment."

She swore under her breath. "I don't know because they are talking, calmly, like two rational people. Honestly, if they're *talking*, it's more than they've done in a very long time. I still want to be there."

"It was that bad?"

"Oh, it was more than bad."

Just then her father looked toward the door, saw them, and gave her a small smile. Glancing back down at her mother, he stood up.

"Here he comes," she muttered. "I'm glad we didn't have to get somebody to bust down the door."

"Me too. Let's take this one step at a time."

The door opened, and she immediately stepped in, not giving her father a chance to stop her or to make Veni leave. And, with that, Reid stayed right on her heels. He wasn't sure what was going on, but it was apparent that Veni didn't either.

"Dad?" she asked, with a questioning expression.

He nodded. "I came to say goodbye."

She stared at him, wordless for a moment. "You knew?"

"Of course," he replied, then frowned at her. "You didn't?"

She shook her head. "No, I didn't know. Not until the

doctors told us today."

"I'm sorry about that. I knew months ago. Years ago, maybe. Her remission was never really a true remission, and she always kept trying new drugs, trying to buy more time. Her cancer never truly went away," he stated, "and I knew that it kept getting worse. I tried to get her to go for more treatment, but she wouldn't."

"Is that why you fought?" she asked hesitantly.

He gave a bark of laughter. "We fought for a lot of reasons. That was one of them, yes. The other was her stealing my work."

There was no objection from her mother. Veni looked past him to where her mother stared at her. Veni asked in shock, "Mom?"

"Yes?"

"You told me that Dad didn't know about the cancer. Plus you told me that Dad wasn't anywhere close in his research."

"He isn't now because, when I took his work from him, … I took it to a whole new dimension. And that's why he's really here—to say goodbye, of course, but also to see where the work is, where my lab reports are, so he can continue it himself."

Veni blinked. "But you told me to ensure nobody ever got it. And you told me that Dad stole your work, not the other way around."

"It wasn't hers in the first place," her father declared, his tone grim. "An awful lot of people back home expect me to return with it."

Veni winced. "Is that fair?"

"Is what fair?" he asked in amazement. "That was my life's work."

"It was also hers," she added gently, "and look where it got her."

He hesitated, frowning at her.

"This research destroyed your marriage, Dad. And it killed her. The cancer was something she could never really accept because it meant downtime from her work."

"I know that." He looked back at his wife, frowning. "She's the one who turned this into a nightmare," he declared bitterly. "As much as I loved her, I didn't love her once I was thrown in jail because my work wasn't as good as hers."

Veni winced at that. "Seriously, that's not what happened, is it?"

"Of course it is," he stated, astonished. "Natalia also knew that jail would quite possibly be the outcome."

"No, I didn't know that," Natalia argued, gasping in pain from the bed. "You had the connections. I didn't. I knew that, if I could do what I needed to do, I could prove to the world that what we were doing worked," she explained, "but it was so slow, and I needed Veni."

At that, she stiffened and glared at her mother. "No, you didn't need me. You wanted me to help, and you wanted me to do whatever it was *you* wanted to do, but you didn't need me."

"I did," Natalia argued. "You made the work go so much easier, so much faster. The results were amazing."

Her father turned to stare at Veni, questions all over his face.

Veni watched as a new potential danger arose. This was where she started to lose her train of thought. "I'm not a scientist in any way, Dad. I've never had anything to do scientifically with any of her work."

He nodded, a look of relief on his face. "That's why I was so confused when they told me that you were here too. I understand why Natalia ran, although not so much once I realized how sick she was, except that she's turned her back on her country again," he snapped, glaring at Natalia. "That is something I find hard to understand as well."

Reid didn't get the undertones here at all. "Why are you here now, sir?" he asked calmly.

At that, the older man turned and glared at him. "Who are you to ask me that question?" he snapped.

"He's a longtime friend of mine, Dad. He's special to me."

Reid put a hand on her shoulder. "It's all right, honey. I don't need defending."

Her father looked from her to him and back again. "He's yours?"

"Yes," she stated immediately. "Whether you like it or not."

He shrugged. "It's important for you to have protection, so that's good, but you're still coming back with me."

"Why is that?" she asked curiously.

Reid was surprised at her response because he expected her to flat-out say no. Obviously she was still after information, and *that* he could not understand.

"Because it's important. Your mother has the work, and I need it. So whatever she's done with it, you need to give it to me."

"And if I don't?" she asked bluntly.

He turned to face her. "You are very much like your mother," he declared, with a level of bitterness that seemed to surprise her.

"So that's a bad thing? Is that what you're saying?"

"It's wrong when you go against your father. You know that I'll be dead if I don't come home with that material."

"Will you?" she asked. "I've certainly been at the butt end of what the Kremlin wants," she pointed out, "and I have no intention of going back to subject myself to that type of abuse."

"It wouldn't be abuse. It never would have been that way if your mother had just followed instructions, but she wouldn't. She refused to cooperate with them, and now I'm here, expected to get that research from her."

"Again, what if you don't?"

He shrugged. "That's a whole different story."

"Yet you're here, which means you don't have to go back," she stated. "You could ask for asylum."

"Like you? *No.* I work for my country. I'm not going against it." When she frowned at that, he added, "I'm not a traitor. That is not who I am. They have been good to me," he said. "They've given me labs. They've given me everything I've needed to do the work I have spent my life on—a life's work that she stole from me," he snapped, turning to glare at his wife.

"Yet you came here to see her," Reid interjected again.

He stiffened at that and then nodded. "She is still my wife," he noted heavily. "And it's important I find out where her material is."

"What happens then?" Veni asked her father. "Even if you have her material, what makes you think you'll duplicate the results?"

"If I have the material, I can at least work on duplicating it," he replied. "They will give me that much of a chance at least."

"That's a pretty slim chance. Do you really want to work

with a government that's only willing to give you that much of a chance?" she asked.

He turned stiffly. "You do not understand loyalty. We made a commitment, and that's important to me. She broke that commitment, both in our marriage and to our government," he shared. "That is not something I can live with."

"We couldn't live with their regulations, restrictions, *abuse*, which is why we're here in England, but you're not. Although technically I guess you are," she said, with a headshake. "Although, how you managed to get here so easily, I don't know."

"I managed because I came with the government's help. I'm allowed to be here, and I'm under diplomatic immunity," he explained. "However, that help will be rescinded if I do not return."

"If you don't return *with her work*, you mean. Isn't that what you're saying?"

"Exactly. So I need that work." He turned and looked at his wife. "But, even now, she won't tell me where it is."

"That's because she wants the work for the wider world," Veni stated. "Not just for the Kremlin."

"I can't help her with that. We signed a contract and took a position of responsibility, of trust, and she broke that contract time and time again. Honestly, if she wasn't already so ill, I don't know what would become of her," he admitted, his tone shaky for the first time. "But, because she is so ill, she gets to walk away once again, free and clear."

His tone alternated between being hurt and being angry, but then that was probably normal, based on what Reid had heard about their marriage.

"And if she does give it to you, then what?" Veni asked her dad.

"Then I can go home, and I can work in my lab again. So, if you have any idea how to get that material, so I can continue her work, then that's only fair. Especially since it was my work to begin with."

Veni looked over at her mother, but she had fallen asleep again. "Yet right now she's asleep, and I don't know if she'll even wake up again, … and that is something I'll have to deal with. We were kidnapped and treated terribly. Hauled from one end of the world to the other, held prisoner, and constantly drugged with God-only-knows what. Then you just get to walk in here, free and clear. I don't even know how to feel about that."

"It has to do with loyalty," he repeated, staring at her. "Something you never seemed to understand. You always hated me, and yet I'm not the bad guy."

"I never hated you. Honestly that was never part of my world. I loved you. I just wished we could have had a relationship without everybody fighting all the time. But no matter how much I want that, even now, it will still not happen."

"It can happen," her dad stated. "Come home. That's all that's needed. You can come home, come work with me," he murmured. "You know that's what the Kremlin wants."

"Why would I do that? You do realize that Mom started to go off her rocker at the end."

He stopped and eyed her hesitantly. "I did wonder. She passed on all kinds of weird mumblings at one point that made several of us stop and look sideways at each other, trying to figure out what she was saying."

"Exactly. And, because of that, whatever you've been told, you can't trust it. I've heard her. She just rambles on and on."

He sat down heavily beside his wife and stared. "I was really hoping that her mental faculties were much stronger, but the cancer appears to have ravaged all of her soul."

"And more," she added. "There is no peace after this."

He looked up at her. "Will you stay here?"

She nodded. "I will."

"Even without your mother?"

"Even without my mother. I've thought of it many times over the years. This is where I went to school. It's where I was the happiest." Her father's gaze went directly to Reid, and she nodded. "Yes, he is part of my past and my future, whether you like it or not."

He shrugged. "It's not as if anybody gets an opinion on the matter, and you were always so independent. Scattered, wary, but always independent. We could never figure out what to do with you. Honestly we should never have been parents. We never saw it at the time, but we just don't have that temperament."

Veni couldn't argue with that because her life had been many, many things, but *easy* hadn't been one of them.

Reid watched the exchange, amazed that Veni had managed as well as she had, after growing up with these two as parents. Yet she was holding her own right now in a pretty impressive way.

She looked around the hospital room. "She clearly doesn't have much longer to live. I'm not even sure that she'll wake up again."

"She needs to," her dad stated abruptly. "I can't go home empty-handed. That ... That will not work out well for me."

"No, it may not," she agreed. "However, you must understand that Mom may not tell you anything anyway, not with her declining mental abilities. Surely you have your own notes from back then."

"Yes, but she apparently did something to move it all forward at an incredible speed," he shared, "and that is what they want from me."

"What if she lied?"

Reid looked over at her, barely keeping his facial expression calm. What was Veni up to? She didn't look at him, staring only at her father.

"What do you mean, *lied*?" her father asked, his tone turning harsh. "The Kremlin spent a lot of money getting things to this point. If she lied, that would not be good."

"And yet isn't that exactly what she would do? She wanted out, not for herself but for me. She didn't want me to spend my life the way she had. She wanted me to be free, to have a better life. Instead of what she had, forced to work crazy hours in the lab, pressured to produce, competitive to the point of insanity. She didn't want that life for me. She wanted to come here in order to get a different life for me, … a better life, and she knew it wouldn't happen without some pull, and that pull was her work. So she sacrificed everything she held dear, including her work, to bring me here."

He stared at her in shock. "Oh, good Lord." He turned his gaze to the sleeping woman. "That is something she would do. She never knew what to do with you. You were this anomaly that she couldn't correlate with her science experiments," he explained. "She was constantly uncertain about what to say, what to do, and often ended up saying the worst things to you, just because she didn't know how to react or how to respond. I often found her in tears because she'd said the wrong thing and had set you off, but then you were so emotional."

He made it sound as if Veni's emotions were the worst thing in the world. Reid could only imagine what her life was like growing up in such a family, where everybody was so analytical, where there was absolutely no room for emotions. Yet she'd been created, conceived at some point in time, so there must have been some drive to perform at that level at times.

Her father continued to speak. "Both of us were completely unprepared to be parents. We should have just aborted the fetus," he declared dispassionately, as if completely forgetting that Veni was right here.

She stared at him and shook her head. "Yeah, maybe you should have," she conceded in a dry tone, "because somehow you guys just didn't quite figure out what made me tick."

He looked at her and shrugged. "We tried, though."

Astonished, she stared back at him. "Did you? Did you really? Did you ever get out of the lab long enough to try?"

He waved his hand. "And there, right there, that's you, with that same old argument again. You need to come up with new arguments, if you want to keep going back to the same old topics," he stated. "We've already disputed the logic on the ones you've come up with so far."

Reid's eyebrows shot up at that. He couldn't imagine what it must have been like for her, but it helped to explain the woman who had wanted no commitment, who had wanted to enjoy life for a little bit, without the intensity and drive that her parents had. It didn't make this time any easier for her, and Reid could see that she was still struggling with her father's words, his completely dispassionate tone.

Was it only because his wife was dying, or was it also about convincing his daughter to go back with him? Was it all about securing the documentation of Natalia's work? Reid felt Veni slip her hand into his and squeeze tightly, as if looking for some stability in a world gone awry. He smiled at her gently. "It's okay. This too shall pass."

At that, she gave a gurgle of laughter. "God, I needed to hear that. It does give you some idea of what my life was like though."

"Indeed," he murmured. "But your future is not limited to that which has gone before. Remember that. You have the ability to make better choices now."

"I made those choices when I came here," she declared. "I'm still standing here, staring at my father's presence, in total shock that he gets to walk around free, yet Mom and I were carted all over as prisoners." That comment got her father's attention once again.

"Yet you're the one who tried to escape. If you hadn't, you would have been treated completely differently. You would've been given compassionate leave to come and say goodbye to your mother, wherever she had ended up."

She didn't respond to that at all but added, "All I can tell you right now is that, in the last few months, she got very strange, very uncertain, and almost fanatical. Yet she always was fanatical to a certain extent."

"She was," her father agreed. "Her work was everything to her. I really admired that."

She swallowed hard, then nodded. "Of course you did. What I can tell you is that her recent work is not stable. It's not anything you can count on. I can give you a copy of a lot of it, up to a few months ago. That's when she started getting even worse. Most of it was just gibberish and went in the garbage," she stated. "Yet I can give you what I have up to that point in time, which was about, I don't know, six months ago."

With that, Reid understood what she was doing. He almost smiled in appreciation of her brilliant move, but it was obvious that she would still have to work the angles for a little bit.

Her father stared at her. "If you would do that," he began hesitantly, "I might be able to call them off."

"That would be very good, if you could," she stated. "I don't want to spend my lifetime looking over my shoulder."

He nodded absentmindedly. "But I need the evidence first," he claimed, looking at her sideways.

"Of course you would," she said in a dry tone. "I don't have a laptop or any way to log into the material at this point," she revealed, "so it'll take a little bit."

"Until it happens, I can't do anything for you."

"What email do you want it sent to?"

Eagerly, he gave her his email address. "Seriously you'll help?"

"Seriously I'll help, but only on the condition that I get to walk free. This is not my fight," she stated, "and honestly, as you can see from Mom's state of mind and her present health situation, she's well-past fighting, and the experimental drugs messed her up these last few months. I wasn't even sure who to talk to about it, but it's obvious that something needed to happen. But how do you make something like that happen when you don't even know who to call on."

"No, of course not," he muttered, turning to look at his wife. "If she would wake up one more time, I could ask her."

"You could, but you also know how secretive she is and how absolutely fanatical she is about her work. She'll tell you anything and everything she wants you to hear but not necessarily the truth."

He stared at Natalia for a long moment. "As much as I hate to admit it, you are correct. She was always a little bit like that."

"A little bit?" Veni repeated, with a headshake. "You've both been like that all my life. There's no *little bit* about it." She looked over at Reid, squeezed his hand again, and asked, "Can you get me a secure laptop?"

"I can," he replied, pulling out his phone. He contacted Anders and explained what he needed.

"Is everything okay in there?" Anders asked. "You've got quite a collection of people watching outside."

"Yeah, so far, and, if you can get me that laptop, we might bring this to an easier conclusion."

"I hope so. I'll be there in five."

Reid didn't dare look out the window, but obviously Anders had seen people standing around outside the hospital, probably not sure whether it was safe to come in or not. When a gentle knock came on the door to Natalia's hospital room, Reid opened it and accepted the laptop from Anders.

Anders looked at the tableau in front of him. "Peaceful?" he whispered in a low tone.

"So far."

"Resolving?"

He nodded. "Yes, but with some interesting twists."

"Got it. I'm right outside in the hallway, if you need me."

"Okay, stay alert."

At that, Anders gave him a sharp look.

"He didn't come alone."

"Of course," he muttered. And, with that, he stepped out of the room. Reid turned and handed the laptop to Veni. "As you requested."

She nodded and sat down beside her mom, then logged in and quickly checked her emails. It was a hunch, but it had paid off, and she had it all. With that confirmation, she looked at her father and said, "Tell me your email address again."

He gave her the address and stood there, not able to see what she was doing, but close enough to ensure that she was doing something productive.

As soon as she sent it, she noted, "Check your phone."

"Where's your phone?" he asked.

"The kidnappers stole it," she stated coolly.

He didn't say anything but pulled out his phone and nodded. "It just came in. Is this the only backup you have?"

"It is, and it's from six months ago, likely the last time Mom was technically in any headspace for this."

The relief on his face was monumental. He hesitated and then said, "Thank you."

She nodded. "I probably won't see you again after this."

"So, you won't be coming back to Russia?" he asked.

"No, I won't. I would rather take a bullet than get put in that position again." He stared at her in surprise, and she nodded vehemently. "Yes, it was that bad, and I have no intention of going through that ever again."

"If you hadn't argued with them and given them such a hard time ..."

"I didn't do anything," she snapped. "So don't go blaming this on me."

He fell silent and then nodded. "I know you probably don't believe me, but we both really, really love you."

"I hope so," she muttered. "It'll be a lonely future for you, unless you do this all over again with some other woman."

"No," he stated immediately. "I certainly won't be reproducing again. It's … It's amazing that we produced you," he added, as he tapped his phone. "Obviously you've turned out pretty well." He walked to his wife, leaned over, and kissed her very gently on the cheek, then whispered something that nobody could quite hear. Then he turned to Reid. "Look after my daughter." With that said, he stepped out of the room and disappeared down the hall.

# CHAPTER 17

VENI DIDN'T KNOW whether she should laugh or cry. She looked over at Reid. "Do you think we're safe?"

He shook his head. "No, I don't."

Her lips firmed, and she nodded. "I don't think he necessarily understands that it's not over. I don't know whether he's involved in the next step or not."

"It doesn't matter at this point," Reid replied, "but we must keep you safe in the meantime. As for your mom, well, I'm afraid she doesn't look as if she'll make it very far from here."

"No, and I don't think she wants to anyway. If she can't be in the lab, she's okay to go," Veni stated. "And that may sound ridiculous, but that's also how she feels about the work she was doing."

"It doesn't matter how it sounds," Reid said. "The important thing is to ensure she doesn't have to suffer at this stage of her life. It's palliative care now," he noted. "I would very much like to get you back to the hotel, but I suspect you want to stay here, don't you?"

She nodded, looking up at him. "It'll be the last time I get to see her. For a while there I wasn't even sure she was still alive."

"I know. I just don't feel that we're out of danger yet."

She stiffened and looked toward the door. "You think

they'll get to us in here?"

"No, but I think the longer we're in here, the more we become sitting ducks, and they have time to set up a plan to take us out. That is not something I would like to see happen."

She winced. "And yet the fact remains that I would hate to see my mother die alone." She could tell from Reid's facial expression that he understood but didn't like it. She smiled. "I promise that I'm not always such a trial."

He laughed. "That's funny. I remember you being quite a trial," he teased. "But that's okay, I was up for it then, and I'm up for it now."

She gave him a tearful smile. "You always were the best part of our relationship," she murmured. "I'm still not happy about what I did."

"You didn't do anything except choose to go your own way, so don't ever be ashamed or upset about that," he declared. "That is a right we all have. And don't say it," he added, when she opened her mouth, interrupting her. "I really don't want to be told what a nice man I am."

She burst out laughing. "And yet it's true."

He rolled his eyes. "I've got other things to think about right now. I'll go talk to Anders and see if we can set up an exit plan from here. You spend whatever time you can with your mom. I know it's almost over."

At that, she immediately walked over and sat down beside her mother. "I hope that we have a little bit more time, but honestly I know you're right. I don't think she'll even make it through the night."

He heard the heavily labored breathing of the woman on the hospital bed and nodded. "I suspect you're correct, and all the more reason to be prepared for a quick exit out of here."

As he went to the door, she called out to him. He turned to her, one eyebrow raised. "Did you mean what you told my father?" He looked at her, puzzled. "About looking after me?"

"Absolutely. I would have looked after you last time too," he shared, flashing her that grin.

"Yet we never saw each other in all the years in between."

"No, but we retained that connection. We continued to email or call over those years. Plus I've become a little bit of a fatalist," he shared. "I believe that, when it's time, it's time, and people cross paths for a reason. You crossed my path, and I got a second chance."

"No," she countered, getting up and walking closer, her arms going around his neck. "*I* got the second chance."

He kissed her hard. "Let's ensure we get out of here safely, so we can both enjoy it," he whispered, with a tender look. "Spend whatever time you can with her. I'll be back in a few minutes."

And, with that, he walked out of the room, leaving her to be with the only loved one she really had.

*No, Veni has you now.* And that thought made his day.

# CHAPTER 18

V ENI HAD BARELY sat back down again, when she heard an odd sound from her mother. She hopped to her feet and leaned over, only to hear a weird rattle, and then she heard nothing.

Complete silence.

She stared breathlessly, waiting for her mother to take another breath, but it never came. She slowly sagged back down, as the enormity of what just happened hit her. They had traveled all this way to find freedom, but her mother had found freedom in a completely different way. Veni bowed her head and let the tears flow.

STANDING OUTSIDE IN the hallway, Anders walked over to Reid. "Her father left under escort, but they left two men behind."

"Do we know where they are?"

"No, not at the moment." He nodded toward the room. "How is she?"

"Pretty shocked. I think the end will be way faster than she's expecting. The bottom line is, I don't trust her father or her mother in terms of the work."

"Veni gave it to him, *huh*?" Anders asked curiously. "I

thought maybe she would have held on to it for her mother's sake."

"She didn't give him all of it. From what I could tell, she gave him earlier stuff, from before Veni started to work with her mother, applying her special gift—trying to keep herself out of it as far as Russia and her father are concerned."

Anders let out a low whistle.

"She also did her best to convince him that her mother had been losing it mentally for the last several months, rendering anything she had claimed about her work patently unreliable and not even fit to record. She downplayed her own role as just going along and trying to shield her mother from the realities of her own mental decline."

"That was a hell of a way to play it. Now if only her father believed her."

"I think in a way he did. Maybe he wanted to, and it did serve his purpose really. It also let him off the hook in the sense that it all may have been too far out of the realm of scientific possibilities. So, Veni gave him enough to send him on his way and to appease the Russian government, but hopefully distanced herself from it in the process."

Anders nodded. "So, now the question is whether the Russians want to get rid of the person who delivered the message."

"Or," Reid added, startling him, "do they want to get rid of the person who may still have copies of it."

"Right. So, if they get rid of Veni, then nobody else has access to anything."

"Exactly. And a sniper would be the logical play."

Anders winced at that. "And hardest for us to find."

Reid added, "I've got law enforcement out there looking already. Jonas had already called in about it once, and I informed him that her father was here. He's pretty pissed off about it, but there's nothing he can do about it because of the diplomatic immunity thing."

"Which is a nice way of the Kremlin saying, *screw you* to MI6, and Jonas knows it."

"Exactly. So back to the sniper thing. If you were a sniper, how would you do it?"

He nodded. "If it was a simple takedown, a sniper would be the perfect answer. It's remote, and even a drone could do it these days," he murmured.

"Exactly, that would be my best guess. She'll be outside, so a simple kill shot—could even be a car accident for that matter. Just tidying up loose ends with some local talent, so who can prove that the Russians were involved and wanted it this way."

"So how do we stop it?" Anders asked.

Reid shrugged. "I'm not sure, but I don't think the father is necessarily a part of it. He said that he would do what he could to get them off her case, but I'm not sure he understands how this game is played."

"He's a scientist, so I doubt it," Anders stated. "He's all about budget money and labs, and, if he's worked only in Russia, then he's not even about budget money, since it's all about results. If you get results, you get what you need. If you don't get results, well, too bad for you. You had your chance."

"Right, no second chances with the Russians, and we both know it all too well."

"Never any second chances," Anders clarified. "I'll talk to Jonas and see if we can get surveillance outside. It would be nice if we could just take down the shooter before it ever gets initiated, and, chances are, the failure would be the end of it."

"Do you think so? We have had dead agents and dead kidnappers and a dead witness or two as well."

"I think the Russians are pushing it on UK soil," Anders replied. "They're just cleaning up in Germany and Kazakhstan," he stated, looking over at Reid. "I know it sounds foolish, but the Russians need something to justify that kind of money, that kind of international incident. Look at the bigger picture. It's not as if Veni would sell that information to somebody. Even if she thought about it, does she know how? The UK government may want it, but, if they are given the same material as the Russians have, then the race is pretty even at this point."

"I don't think the Russians particularly like it *even* though," Reid noted, with a wry look.

"No, I'm sure they don't."

"So let's be safe, rather than sorry."

Anders nodded. "Agreed."

The hospital room door opened behind them just then. Reid spun to see Veni staring up at him, wordless and almost dazed, and he knew instantly. "Aww, sweetheart." He opened his arms, and she bailed into them, crying in great big, noisy sobs. He looked over at Anders, who nodded and quickly disappeared. Reid held her close and just rocked her.

Nurses moved into the room, after seeing Veni come out.

When she finally had a chance to calm down and to breathe, she looked up and whispered, "She never even woke up again."

He nodded. "Yet she got to see you at the end, and she got to see her husband. Whether that's right or wrong, it's probably all she could do, and that was her time."

Veni sniffled. "I still had no idea, and yet my father did."

"I suspect they kept in touch to a certain extent. Although there was a lot of anger between them and animosity from their work, there was also love."

"What kind of a love is that? To steal the other's work? To deceive and betray each other every chance they got?"

"Truth be told, it was probably a collaboration to some degree because, like it or not, they did a lot together, and how do you divide up something like research and lab tests when a marriage splits?"

Her lips twitched. "I guess you don't. You just sit there and have ugly recriminations for the rest of time."

"Maybe," he murmured.

She looked up and asked, "Can we leave now?"

He nodded. "Anders is checking to see if it's safe."

"My father left with the lab work. Shouldn't that be enough?"

"We're hoping so," he murmured, "but we can't be certain yet."

She shrugged. "Now that he has the material, I don't think the Russians care beyond that."

"What if you still had a copy of it though?"

She pondered that and shrugged. "They always believed that they're superior in every way. So, as long as they have the same material, they rest assured that they can get to the end result faster than anyone else."

He chuckled. "If that's the case, we may be good to go." Then he ushered her toward the exit, sending Anders a text that they were coming out.

As they approached the front door, a vehicle pulled up right to the door, up on the walkway even. She looked at the driver and confirmed, "That's Anders."

"Yep, we're taking you to a hotel for now, and then we'll have to reestablish where and what we're to do with this mess."

"*Great.*" She shuddered, leaning against him. "I don't even know how to feel anymore."

"I understand, but it's not today's issue," he stated. "Today is just about recovery. It's about figuring out and honoring your mother for who she was at the best of times, setting aside the other times, the secrets, the lies. There's enough of those kinds of things in the world, so nobody needs to remember them."

She squeezed his hand again. "I know you don't like it when I say it."

"Don't—" he warned, with a smile in his tone.

"You're still a really nice man."

He winced as that hit home. "The insults, oh, the insults."

She burst out laughing. "You're such a ham," she muttered. "I forgot about that sense of humor of yours."

"Seems to me that you've forgotten an awful lot."

"I did," she admitted, "but that's okay because you will remind me."

He opened the front door cautiously, checking his surroundings. He saw several other men moving through the hospital complex, separating, going into individual buildings. He moved her quickly to the passenger side of the vehicle.

She frowned. "From the way you're moving, you're expecting an attack."

"Let's just say that I'm not sure that we're out of danger," he replied. "The Russians have a tendency to clean up loose ends."

"Maybe so, but I don't know anything. We don't know

that anybody would care at this point."

"The news isn't out yet that your father has her research. Plus the Russians don't even know that your mother's gone, not to mention that you're not a scientist and don't know what to do with her work anyway. Then there's the fact that it was probably written in Russian anyway."

She nodded. "Because that was my mother's first language, although born and raised in the UK, my grandfather insisted on our learning the language."

As he gave her a boost into the seat, he added, "Scooch over, and I'll come in behind you."

*Crack!*

Shouts from both Anders and Reid filled the air, as the vehicle lurched forward, almost leaving Reid flat on the sidewalk, but he was still hanging on to the side, with her screaming in the back seat. He quickly propelled himself inside and slammed the door shut. "Are you okay?" he yelled at Anders.

He nodded, his face grim. "Yeah. Didn't see that one coming. He took out the front windshield though."

"*Great,*" she muttered from the back seat. "I always wanted a better view."

He looked into the rearview mirror and smiled at her. "Hang tight."

Several other shots rang out in the parking lot, as they swerved to get out and around the hospital parking, shouts coming from everybody all around. Anders hit the brakes, due to all the cars stopped before him, then saw a fight on a nearby rooftop.

The shouting was off the charts, both here on the ground and also on that rooftop. Then one of guys, with a big rifle slung on his back, jumped over the edge and fell to his death.

# CHAPTER 19

"**D**EAR GOD," VENI whispered, watching the man fall to the ground from several stories up. "Why?" she cried out.

"Because going home as a failure was not an option," Reid whispered calmly. "But now, with any luck, that should put an end to it." He looked over at Anders, as if asking his opinion.

Anders nodded. "I would think so, at least for the moment. We can get the governments on it from now on." And, with that, he backed up, got around the multitude of vehicles clogging up amid the chaos and slowly pulled the vehicle forward.

"Is it safe to drive like this, without a windshield?" she asked.

"Safe enough, but, once we get settled, we'll switch out vehicles again."

"Good," she muttered, "I hope we're safe now."

"I think it's over," Reid suggested.

She smiled up at him and asked, "Like *over*-over?"

"Really *over*-over," he said, with a chuckle. "The governments can sort it out from here on out."

"Great," she muttered.

"You know that our government will also expect a copy of that material, right?"

She nodded. "I know. I'll give them exactly the same copy I gave my father." When he looked at her in surprise, she shrugged. "The lab work without anything to do with me."

"Ah." Reid nodded. "That makes sense."

"I don't want anybody else yanking my chain, the way my mother kept trying to do," Veni admitted. "It's one thing if I choose to go into a lab and do the work, trying to find something that I can apply my skills to. It's another thing to be forced into it."

"Understood," Reid confirmed, "and Terk and I will back you the whole way."

She smiled. "At least Terk's name seems to get some response from people."

Anders chuckled from the front seat. "You have no idea. Almost everybody in this industry owes Terk for their lives at one time or another," he shared, with a shrug. "We're all indebted to him."

"Yet he probably doesn't want that at all," she murmured.

Reid looked at her in surprise and asked, "How do you know?"

She shrugged. "From you. From what you keep telling me. When you guys do this kind of work, and you have this kind of skill, I can't imagine that anybody wants to be thanked for it. It's more a case of just *Go away and leave us alone.*"

He burst out laughing, understanding that totally, but he nodded too. "Terk is kind of reclusive."

"Of course he is," she stated, with a smile.

As they walked down the hallway to their new hotel room, they found the door partially open. Reid immediately tucked her behind him and pushed the door wide as he stepped in.

Somebody sat in the living room, a cup of coffee in his hand, talking on his phone.

Reid frowned at him. When he ended the call, he asked, "Riff? You're back?"

Riff assessed the two of them, then smiled. "I'm escorting you home."

She stepped forward, staring at him. "Where is home?"

"Home is at Terk's place," he shared. "Both of you get to report to Terk after this."

"What if we don't want to?" she asked, frowning at him.

"Then don't, but I'm pretty sure you'll find out that you're more than eager to be there."

"Why is that?" she asked.

"Because Terk and I are like you two," Riff murmured, with a smile. "And there's nothing quite like knowing you are accepted where your home is, where you can grow and where you're protected," he added, with emphasis.

She sighed. "But do you think he'll let me come? It's not as if I can do much."

Riff burst out laughing. "If you would have opened up your end of the psychic communication pathway at all, you would realize Terk's been talking to you the whole time. You just haven't been listening very well."

"I did hear somebody earlier," she admitted. "I thought I was either losing my mind or that maybe it was another prisoner."

"It *was* another prisoner," Riff confirmed. "Terk sent me in to get him out from under the Russian influence. He's recuperating at Terk's right now."

"Seriously?" she asked, staring at him in delight. "You

mean, I did some good?"

He nodded. "You did a lot of good, and that's another reason why Terk would like to see you. You have an open invitation to join them," he said, with a smile. "I just tend to be a little more direct about it, but it is your decision." He looked over at Reid. "Nice job, by the way. Now you guys are off the hook, and we can get you home again."

Reid stepped forward and asked, "Was that you dealing with the sniper?"

Riff just smiled.

Reid nodded, then asked, "What about Anders?"

Anders stepped in behind him. "I've already got my orders," he shared. "I'm heading home on the next flight. Riff's taking over from here."

"Sounds good to me," Reid said. "Thanks for your help, Anders."

Anders smirked. "Anytime for family."

Riff stood and stretched, looking around. "You got any food here?"

"No, not yet, but feel free to get some," Veni suggested, as she walked in and collapsed on a chair. "I'm exhausted. I need a bath, and I need some sleep. I'm not leaving until I deal with my mother's body."

"What is it you want to do about her burial?" Reid asked curiously.

She frowned. "Honestly, back to Russia is where she would want to be."

"Then we'll arrange that," Reid stated, "but you won't go for a service or funeral or anything inside Russia. We can contact your father and have him take care of the details."

"Yeah, do that," she said. "As crazy and twisted as their relationship was, … I know she still loved him, and he loved her."

And, with that, Riff announced, "Okay, I'll check in with Jonas, so he can make arrangements for your mother's body to be taken back. While I'm waiting for his confirmation, I'll go roust up some food. Again, you understand you won't go to her funeral or anything. Being there is far too high of a risk, and we would strongly advise against it."

"I understand, and that's fine. I got to see her alive, and that's … far more than I thought I would get, honestly."

Riff nodded, then looked at the two men, still standing here, staring at him. "I'll be a couple hours." And, with that, he was gone.

Anders looked over at Reid. "Do you want me to stay until he's back?"

Reid immediately shook his head. "No, we're good. It's over, and we need to discuss what we'll do from here," he shared, looking over at Veni, who had collapsed in the chair, staring out into space.

Anders nodded. "In that case," he said, with a smack on Reid's shoulder, "I'll see you next time." And, within minutes, he was gone too.

Reid sat down beside her and pulled her into his arms. Almost as if that unlocked the dam, she burst into tears.

It was a while before she looked up at him, her sobs finally quieting down to just a gentle hiccup, and she murmured, "I know you don't like me to say it."

"So don't," he replied, laughing at her. "You needed that. I mean, not everybody loses a parent on the same day they gain freedom from a regime."

She sniffled and nodded. "To think that she knew about her cancer and didn't tell me. I don't know what to do with that."

"And that's a betrayal or a secret or whatever you end up calling it that you'll have to accept somehow," he stated gently. "But she did what she felt was right *for you*. She did all she could to protect you."

"Of course. Isn't that what every parent says to their child?" she muttered, with a headshake.

"Often, yes," he agreed, with a smile. "Now, do you want to shower? I don't know how quickly we're leaving once Riff gets back, so …"

She looked at her watch. "I'm not going anywhere tonight. I'm exhausted."

"Good enough, but food is coming, so maybe take a shower and then have a nap. He did say he would be a couple hours."

"And I've eaten into that with all that crying," she muttered, as she got up. "But, yes, a shower would be good."

She headed to the bathroom and turned on the hot water. When he walked in behind her, she smirked and asked, "What's the matter? Now you don't trust me in the shower alone?"

"I don't want you to fall. I don't want you to break down in tears again. So, if you're okay …" And he looked at her hesitantly.

"I'm fine," she murmured, with a wave of her hand. "But feel free to join me if you want. You probably need a shower too."

His eyebrows shot up, and she knew she'd surprised him.

REID CHUCKLED. "I wanted to take it slow. I had no idea

this was going from zero to sixty quite so fast, but—"

"I'm totally okay to go from zero to sixty. I know it sounds cheesy, but how about zero to forty-five or maybe zero to ninety?" she asked coyly. "It's been a hell of a long week, and it's not even over, and we'll be moving in with strangers." She shrugged. "So I'm feeling a little bit … I don't know how I feel. I guess I'm uncertain about it all."

"So, you think making love will make a difference?"

She shook her head, laughing. "To that? No, hell no. But to the way I'm feeling on the inside? Absolutely," she murmured, as she walked closer, the shower filling the bathroom with steam behind her. "The thing is, we don't always get what we want in life, and sometimes, even when we do get it, we don't really see it as being the way we wanted it."

She added, "So it becomes a case of take what you can, yet make the most of it. That has been a lesson that I've learned this week. Seeing you again after all this time?" She shook her head. "It's been amazing, and I really, really, really love the fact that you're back in my life. But I have to admit that it feels that something is missing."

"What's that?" he asked, looping his arms around her lower back and tugging her closer.

"This," she whispered, as she reached up and kissed him gently.

By the time she slipped back, he was already humming at the sixty mark and looking down at her with a glazed expression.

"That's right," she said. "Remember that part."

He grinned. "I did, but we didn't get a chance to explore that side of our relationship very often."

"No, not very often. But, when we did get together, it

was dynamite," she murmured. "Now, that shower is waiting for me, and you can bet I won't let the hot water go to waste."

And right in front of him, she stripped down to the skin and stepped in the shower. He was two seconds behind her, dropping his clothing into a heap, sending mental messages to Riff to ensure he was slow as hell coming back with food.

*You've got a couple hours, and I'll give you a warning before I come in.*

Reid chuckled, as he stepped under the water.

She frowned at him. "Riff talks telepathically?" She immediately flushed. "Oh, my gosh, I totally forgot he's coming back."

"Let's just say that I told him to take his time."

She looked at him in delight, threw her arms around him, and muttered, "Perfect. Time is what we need. Maybe a nice long hot shower and a nap would be perfect," she suggested, waggling her eyebrows.

"As if you'll have a nap," he teased.

"I might," she declared, "depending on how much you exhaust me."

And, with that, she launched herself at him again, wrapping her arms tightly around his neck and plastering her body to his, from chest to thigh, skin to skin, the heat instantly surging between them. She wiggled several times, trying to get closer. When he finally lifted her and pinned her up against the shower wall, she chuckled. "I think we did it this way before too."

"We might have," he murmured against her throat, his hands busy caressing her thighs, then back to her plump butt. He murmured, "I ... I'm so overwhelmed with emotions right now that my memories are a little thin on the ground."

"That's because it's all about sensations," she whispered, as she wiggled deeper into his hands. "Yet you could hurry this up a bit."

"I don't want to hurry anything up," he shared. Yet he positioned her a little bit higher, her thighs spread and wrapped around his hips, with him right at the heart of her.

"Yes," she whispered.

And, with that, he drove in as hard and as deep as he could. Then he stilled and shuddered in place. She closed her eyes and moaned. "Dear God," she said, among her whimpers. "After everything we've been through, who would have thought this would feel quite so nice."

"Well, *me* for one," he replied, chuckling. "I can't say this ever feels bad with you."

And he started to move again, sending water splashing everywhere, as it crashed down on top and all around them, as he thoroughly made love to her. By the time she exploded in his arms, he was cresting on his own wave and crashing back down to Earth. Yet still not even back to Earth. It was like finding a halfway station, where nothing quite seemed real anymore.

She looked up at him and whispered, "God, I'd forgotten."

He shifted her position ever-so-slightly and asked, "Do you want me to turn off the water?"

"No," she whispered, as she put her arms around his neck. "I want to do that again."

He laughed. "Sounds good to me."

He gave her a moment to rest and then started to drive deeper and deeper. She cried out in his arms several more times, before he allowed himself another climax. By that time, they had turned off the water, as it had run cold.

SHE CHUCKLED, AS she stepped out of the shower. "I wasn't thinking I could sleep. Yet right now? … I'm kind of tired."

"Or do you need food first?" he asked. "I can have Riff come back with the food."

"That might be a good idea." She frowned at him. "You really can talk to him telepathically, can't you?"

"I can," he said cheerfully. "So can you. You just have to open that door in your mind."

"What if I don't want to?" she asked mutinously.

"Then don't," he said, gently looking over at her. "Your time frame, your decision. You get to be comfortable in what you can do and when you want to do it. It's your choice."

She sighed. "Okay, fine. That sounded very foolish on my part." She opened the door in her mind and called out, *Riff, the coast it clear. It's safe to come back again. Bring food.*

His tone was clear as a bell, when he replied, *Good thing because I'm walking up the stairs right now, and I am bringing food. Ensure you're all dressed when I get there.*

Laughing, she relayed the message to Reid, and he nodded. "I heard," he said, as he leaned over and kissed her hard. "Now, let's not make the poor man blush."

She chuckled. "I don't think he would blush that easily."

"Doesn't matter. We'll have to learn a whole new way of communicating between ourselves, blocking out the others."

And, with that, they quickly dressed, and, by the time Riff walked in with hot food, they were sitting here, waiting for him.

"Glad to see you guys have worked out a few issues,"

Riff announced. "Any problems with going home now that your father will oversee your mother's funeral in Russia?"

She shook her head. "No, but obviously we need to talk to Terk."

"You need time to recuperate and rest," Riff noted, "so I suggest you do that all at Terk's place."

"Sounds good to me," she said, with a yawn. "Although it seems fairly intimidating to be working with people who are so much more talented."

Riff shrugged. "Everybody there is incredibly talented. Even a few people who didn't have abilities when they started are slowly developing some."

"People without abilities are there?" she asked in surprise.

He nodded. "Not all partners came with abilities," he shared with a smile, "and it didn't matter in the least. You'll be welcomed for who you are and what you are, which is as a person. So don't expect anything less, and you'll be treated just fine."

"I never expected anything differently," she noted. "I've heard such amazing things about Terk."

"And they're all true, dammit," Riff agreed, then burst out laughing. "In fact, he's listening in on this conversation as well."

"I'll have to learn to tell when he is and when he isn't," she murmured, "because it's all new to me."

*Not that new*, Terk replied. *You managed to talk to me just fine. You'll find your abilities will grow incredibly, once you get here. Everybody's have.*

She smiled at Reid, reaching out to hold his hand. "I can't wait."

# EPILOGUE

S ANDERS OPENED HIS eyes, feeling the shudders rippling through his body. Once again one of the female healers was at his bedside. "Will I live?" he asked, a note of humor in his tone.

"You'll definitely live," she declared, "but I'm hearing rumors that some people may not be very happy that you escaped their custody."

He winced at that. "Will that cause you guys trouble?"

"That's not your problem," she stated firmly. "Your problem is making sure you're healthy."

"I'm doing much better," he noted. "I was thinking I could get up and come down for a meal."

"If you feel you're up to it, then do so." She eyed him carefully. "However, just a few minutes ago, you didn't seem to be up for it."

"I'm feeling much better now," he said.

She nodded. "I'll give you ten minutes to get dressed, and then I'll walk you down to ensure you're okay and can find your way."

"Is it that bad?"

"It's that bad," she confirmed, with a laugh to lighten the truth.

She closed the door behind her, and he quickly dressed in the clothing the women had provided for him. He had no idea where he was or when he got here. He knew this place was huge, and lots of people were here. They'd been looking after him since his rescue, but he didn't even know who all these people were. When he opened the door, she studied him carefully and nodded.

"You look like you're holding for the moment."

"Thanks," he said. "I was trying not to burn through too much energy."

"No, never a good idea," she agreed comfortably, as she walked downstairs at his side. When they entered this massive room with the largest table he'd ever seen in his life, all the conversations stopped. Veni raced to his side. Grateful, he enclosed her in a warm hug.

Terk stood and walked over to him. "Sanders, how're you doing?"

"Considering what I've been through, I think I'm doing just fine." He reached out a hand, and shook Terk's. "I didn't get a chance to say it before, but thank you."

"You're welcome. Riff is the one who rescued you."

Sanders nodded at Riff, seated at the table. Then Sanders turned back to Terk. "Now, if only there was a way to go back and rescue somebody else."

At that, Terk frowned. "What do you mean, somebody else?"

"One of my jailers, his daughter has abilities, like us. She doesn't dare tell anybody, of course," he shared. "When she realized what I could do, we stayed in contact the whole time, without telling anybody, just to keep her safe, but she's desperate to get out of there."

"Where you were being held? Up north?"

"Yes, but her father moved her to the Baltic Sea area."

He nodded. "Do you think that *you*'ll go back and get

her?" Terk asked.

Sanders winced. "If I can have another couple days to get my strength up, that would be ideal. I can't leave her behind, and I feel that I don't have much time to do that."

"How old is this daughter?" Clary asked.

He looked over at her. "Twenty-seven."

"So, she's not a child anymore."

"No, and she's lived in fear all her life. Her abilities are pretty strong. Apparently her mother did her best to keep them hidden, but her mother was killed a few months back, and her father's gotten more and more suspicious."

"Of course. Any strong gift like that will be revealed, and, although she's probably been good at keeping it contained, she's obviously slipped a time or two."

"Exactly, and I know her father. I also know that everybody there was looking for more psychics, and, if her father thought that he could curry favor by providing a bona fide one, his position in the guard would be gold."

"What about his daughter? Does she want to leave her father?" Clary asked.

"Her father's the problem. Her mother is now gone, and, although he's been a good father, I think she's afraid he would give her up in a heartbeat to elevate his own position. Don't forget that, for these Russians, it's a point of honor. It's not a case of thinking that she would be hurt because, from his point of view, she would be in an exalted position as being special. She would be a *special* prisoner," he explained. "In her father's mind, as a female, she would always be somebody's prisoner, but he wouldn't call it *prisoner*. He would call it *their wife*."

"Ah, right." Clary winced. "God, I hate that mind-set."

"You might hate it, but it's prevalent in those patriarchal

societies," Sanders said. "So I would very much appreciate a chance to build up my strength a bit and then get her out of there."

"Do you think you'll be up against much opposition?" Terk asked.

"It depends on whether her father has found out what she can do or not," Sanders replied, "but, in my heart, I would say, *absolutely*."

"Why is that?" Terk asked. "Have you had any contact with her?"

He hesitated and then shook his head. "No, not since I was rescued. She cried out for me to run and to ensure that I got free and clear. When I asked her to come with me, she said that she was hurt, and she couldn't right then. No way she could get out at the time."

"So, presumably she is still there then."

"I told her that I would come back for her," Sanders shared. "No way I can just leave her."

"I get that," Clary replied, as she looked over at Riff. "You up for heading back to that lovely region?"

"It's Estonia, so it's beautiful, cold in the winter, but it's a gorgeous part of the world. If she's there, we would have a much easier time getting her out because we would have the sea available." He looked over at Terk and shrugged. "I'm game."

"In that case, Sanders, get your strength back up, ensure you're grounded with somebody here, and we'll set up a plan to rescue her. And if she has abilities …"

"She does, very strong abilities," Sanders confirmed. "I'm just not sure they are things you can use."

"What do you mean?"

"She's a mind reader. She can look at you and repeat

what you're thinking. But it's more than that. It's almost as if she can see different layers of you."

Terk stared at him, his head tilted to the side. "We certainly have various abilities here," he began, "but we've never seen that before. Still, it doesn't mean that's how it would stay either. The longer we all cohabitate in one place, the more we're becoming adept at hiding our personal feelings from the others, working through multiple conversations in our head at once, learning what privacy means among psychics, while gaining more gifts," he shared. "So, if she's got another ability for us to adapt to, I say bring it on." He looked around at the others.

"If she's in trouble, and she needs help," Clary stated, "I say, go get her."

"Exactly," her sister, Cara, agreed. "We came here because we were looking for a safe place to be *us*. So anybody else who needs a safe place to be themselves should be welcome too."

And, with that, everybody agreed.

Terk looked over at Sanders. "Looks like you're it. Give yourself three or four days, and you should be ready to go."

"With a little bit of help from the ladies here," he replied, "I would like to be ready to go in two." He looked at Cara and Clary.

They both nodded. "If she's in trouble, absolutely," they said in unison. "Plan to be out of here by then." They turned and looked at Riff. "Are you good with that?"

"Absolutely. Those bellies of yours are getting bigger, and I know Angela's on her way to deal with you and the other pregnant ladies. I sure don't want to be around when Angela shows up."

"We haven't forgotten our promise to you either," Terk

pointed out. "We will find out who murdered your fiancée."

He stiffened at that. "I knew you hadn't forgotten. I just figured that we still don't have anything to go on."

"No, not yet," Terk agreed, "but not for lack of trying."

"I know. If it were that easy, I would have solved it already," he murmured, looking around at the people at the table. "I appreciate that you're all still trying."

With that said, Riff got up and walked out the door.

This concludes Book 6 of Terk's Guardians: Reid.
Read about Sanders: Terk's Guardians, Book 7

# Terk's Guardians: Sanders
# (Book #7)

Sanders hadn't been expecting a rescue from his own captivity. Now free, he can do no less than help Ania, another captive, someone he barely knows. Yet his connection to her had kept Sanders alive during his darkest times. He can do no less than help her now.

Ania must escape her father's total control. However, during Ania's first few days in confinement, her head had to clear of the drugs her father had been feeding her, just to keep her compliant and captive. After missing a dose, clarity now returning, Ania finally understands and bolts. But where can she go? She has no one. Until Sanders reaches out …

Meanwhile her father had put a psychic tracker on Ania's tail. Now Sanders and Ania try to hide, yet must find each other, … before her father locates them both.

Find Book 7 here!
To find out more visit Dale Mayer's website.
https://geni.us/DMSSanders

# Author's Note

Thank you for reading Reid: Terk's Guardians, Book 6! If you enjoyed the book, please take a moment and leave a short review.

Dear reader,

I love to hear from readers, and you can contact me at my website: www.dalemayer.com or at my Facebook author page. To be informed of new releases and special offers, sign up for my newsletter or follow me on BookBub. And if you are interested in joining Dale Mayer's Reader Group, here is the Facebook sign up page.
http://geni.us/DaleMayerFBGroup

Cheers,
Dale Mayer

# About the Author

Dale Mayer is a *USA Today* best-selling author, best known for her SEALs military romances, her Psychic Visions series, and her Lovely Lethal Garden cozy series. Her contemporary romances are raw and full of passion and emotion (Broken But … Mending, Hathaway House series). Her thrillers will keep you guessing (Kate Morgan, By Death series), and her romantic comedies will keep you giggling (*It's a Dog's Life*, a stand-alone novella; and the Broken Protocols series, starring Charming Marvin, the cat).

Dale honors the stories that come to her—and some of them are crazy, break all the rules and cross multiple genres!

To go with her fiction, she also writes nonfiction in many different fields, with books available on résumé writing, companion gardening, and the US mortgage system. All her books are available in print and ebook format.

## Connect with Dale Mayer Online

*Dale's Website – www.dalemayer.com*
*Twitter – @DaleMayer*
*Facebook Page – geni.us/DaleMayerFBFanPage*
*Facebook Group – geni.us/DaleMayerFBGroup*
*BookBub – geni.us/DaleMayerBookbub*
*Instagram – geni.us/DaleMayerInstagram*
*Goodreads – geni.us/DaleMayerGoodreads*
*Newsletter – geni.us/DaleNews*